METAMERISM

STORIES OF BECOMING

APRIL STEENBURGH

For Laura Anne.

INTRODUCTION

When I was very little, I was fascinated with stories about werewolves.

I stayed fascinated as I grew, especially when I discovered there were *other* were-creatures and shapeshifters. I grew up wondering what it would be like to be something else, to be *other*. As a young queer tomboy trying to make my skin fit, as opposed to itch, and then as a much older non-binary witch, the idea that one could change, slip a skin and be something else, felt important. Something that settled deep down into the bones. A hopeful thing. The dream that something better is coming, even if we have to fight for it. Change and transformation were not only possible, they were essential.

There is an entire academic paper in the connection between identity and shapeshifting mythology. We need these stories. We learn from these stories.

The first story I published was about a selkie — you can find it in The Modern Fae's Guide to Surviving Humanity. My second was about a were-crow, found in the Were- collection by ZNB. That held breath, the liminal space of coming-into-being, has always seeped into my writing. I knew it was there, but I had not really looked at how persistent it was. It took bringing so many separate projects together to notice the pattern. Changing. Moving. Coming-into-being. Learning. Taking action.

From the werewolves and selkies that caught my heart as a child to witches and the hard choices we make—I hope you enjoy looking at these moments of change.

BED TIME STORIES

When I was young, my sister made a wolf. It was almost a game. I would lay still, listening to the creak of the floors as they dutifully reported the location of our parents. When those creaks were far enough away, across our seemingly endless ranch-style house, I would slip out from my covers, and out the door of my room— just another shadow cast by the hallway nightlight if my parents had looked down the hall.

My sister was older, and as such I assumed wiser and powerful. So when I slipped into her blankets and rested my head on her chest, I listened avidly as she described her wolf. If I closed my eyes, just to the point where everything was blurred by eyelash and restricted by the curve of eyelid, I could see him as she spoke in her quiet, determined voice, describing him, drawing him for me with words.

He was a young wolf, lanky and long limbed, but his breath was warm as he sniffed at me, as my sister told him about me just as much as she told me about him. There was not wet dog smell, no click of nails on the floor. That was the sort of thing best left to domestic canines. He smelled like rolling in the dirt on a hot day, like somewhere just far enough away to long for. His fur as he brushed past was coarse. It made me shiver with a mix of terror and excitement. I never opened my eyes, not fully, to look. The one time I cracked them open wide enough to peek through my lashes, I saw two bright eyes far too close to my own. It felt like a violation, a breach of trust, as I met those eyes.

I never did that again.

Each night I snuggled in close, listened to my sisters soft, excited voice, as she described her wolf. As she described how he was, who he was. I listened for years. We were close, the two of us. Even as she grew more into a young woman and I straggled after her as a young girl. She always had time for me, a smile, a hug, and a whispered story about her wolf.

But as she stepped close to adulthood she went sort of sideways, sort of strange, and did not leave even a twisty path for me to follow. The strange started as the shape of our Wolf visits changed. She would drift off, stopping mid-sentence. Sometimes she would pick back up, her voice thick with an emotion I could not quite put a name to. Other times I would wait, heartbeat loud in my ears, for her to speak. When she stopped like that, lost somewhere in her words, I would be met with the inevitable "goodnight, Allie." A dismissal that sent me back to my own bed, tail between my legs, not quite sure what I had done.

Days were easier. Whatever it was that sent her attention wandering seemed lighter when the sun was up. It was still there, I would catch her staring off to space when she should have been doing homework and every now and then I would startle her into dropping whatever it was she had been holding just by asking her a question. She was listening to something I could not quite hear, and I hated feeling that distance between us. I wriggled in as close as I could get, holding space for me in her space. I was determined to keep that space open for me, reassuring and reminding us both with touch and heartbeat and soft breathing. Grabbing her hand as we walked together to get the mail. Tickling her as we sat together watching television. Singing off key and loud when she was trying to listen to one of her favorite songs. *I am here*, I was shouting. Pay attention to me. Tell me stories. Write me into your story.

But it wasn't until I went to slip into her room one night when I was older, probably too old to acceptably snuggle in bed with a sibling, and found the door closed, that the strange seemed cruel and final. Locked. Lexi had never shut me out before. Ever. I stood there long enough to get cold in my sleep pants, t-shirt, and bare feet. I knocked then, as a shiver shook me.

She did not answer. But I could smell warm earth and a bit of grass and wildflower as I stood there and I knew she was visiting with her wolf. I felt left out. Abandoned and rejected and I ran back to my room before the tears welling in my eyes could fully blind me, before the sob that was ratcheting tension through my chest could snap free. But he knew, her wolf. He could have smelled the sorrow and anger on me and that curdled everything into a ball of shame in my stomach. If her wolf could know, she would know. For the first time in my life I hated my own vulnerability.

Things seemed no different than they had ever been come morning, at least not for Lexi. I was the one with shadows under my eyes and prickling under my skin. She had her same pre-shower mess of hair complete with dramatic cowlick as she shambled into the kitchen to beg a cup of coffee off of Mom.

"You're too young"

"Seriously? I am seventeen. How can I *still* be too young?"

"Tam. Just let the girl have some coffee." Dad's voice from the den.

"See? Dad says its ok."

Lexi was smug up until Dad followed his statement with "she'll hate it anyway."

The pieces were all there, I just couldn't make them fit right anymore. There was a buzzing just under the familiar noise of a Saturday morning. An anxiousness. It was hard for me to focus. I spilled my cereal, tripped over nothing, and made a general nuisance of myself until mom finally snapped for me to go outside before I took the house down in my clumsy fumbles.

The odd jarring sense of things being out of place eased in the light of the day, as time collected between me and that locked door. The dissonance had vanished by dinner, when Lexi offered to take my turn at doing dishes. And since it was an uncomfortable sensation that had plagued me through the night and into the morning, I buried it deep where I wouldn't have to notice it. I smothered it beneath the familiar comfort of Lexi's smile, Dad's gruff humor, Mom's rolled eyes. I was just imagining things.

Lexi's door remained locked to me. I found myself standing in the hall one night, a whimper trying to pry its way out of my tight throat. I did not know what I had done. I was afraid that Lexi was beyond my reach, that the tether that had always been so strong between us was strained to the point of snapping. I did whimper then, a faint and strangled sound sharp with panic and desperation. *I am here. Pay attention to me. Write me into your story. Don't leave me. Don't leave me behind.*

The sound cut off when I thought I caught an answering sound from behind that door. A huff of air, a soft thump of paw pads on the floor. Warm earth and cut grass and wildflowers. Wolf.

I scrambled back across the hall to my room, closing my door and wishing I, too, had a lock. I huddled under my blankets and whimpered once more. And something answered.

Damp soil. Crushed grass. A huff of warm, moist breath on my cheek. I opened my eyes and went still. Green eyes bright in the darkness of the room, a powerful, lanky form with a thick gray coat I could just see by the light of my mushroom-shaped nightlight. Wolf. *My* wolf.

I wanted so much to scoot back across the hall, excitement propelling me with a speed only the young can manage. I wanted to show my sister my wolf, pride carrying every word as I shaped him for her. I wanted my sister to see that I was grown up and she did not have to leave me behind after all. But I knew that door would be closed. Tears of frightened abandonment warmed into tears of anger. Sisters can be fierce, petty things. Lexie did not want to share her wolf? Then she would not get to meet mine.

His breath was warm as he sniffed at me, filling himself with my scent and seeming to grow more real with every inhalation. I reached out as I had never dared to do with Lexi's wolf, and ran a hand down his side as he moved past me. Coarse and thick, his coat was glorious. A tingle of something like static and something like nerves jolted through me and I felt myself almost panting as I began to whisper, to shape him in the darkness. Eventually the line between dream and consciousness became blurred beyond recovery and I slept.

When I woke that morning and made my sleepy stumbling way down the hall to the kitchen, I found my parents sitting at the table, their coffee so old and cold it no longer filled the air with its welcoming scent. They looked miserable. Mom's phone was sitting in front of her, face up, and she stared at it as if willing it to light up with an incoming call.

"Mom?"

Dad looked at me, the smile that unfolded on his face was a forced and sickly thing. It had teeth. His upper lip curled back as the smile lost its shape and faltered into a grimace. "Allie. Good morning."

The body language of adults is important to a child. We learn how to act, and react, from those around us. There was tension in every inch of my parents, unhappiness tangled up in every shift and gesture. It sent worry screaming down every nerve and soured my stomach. "What happened?"

"Lexi has moved out." Mom turned over her phone turning the face to the table. I flinched at the finality contained in the soft thud her phone made. I grimaced at the taste of the lie. It was sharp, shockingly bitter and it dried up my mouth so that I needed to find something, anything, to drink to wash that taste away.

"She moved out?" The words came out thick, making me sound sleepier than I was, confused, as I made my way to the sink, turned on the faucet, and drank directly in the way my mother absolutely hated.

"Allie. Stop that. We are not animals. Yes, she moved out. She left this morning."

Lie. It raised a ghost of hackles across my neck. I wiped my mouth and looked at my mother. I remembered the way Lexi's wolf had regarded me, unblinking, looking through me. There must have been some of that in my eyes as mom looked away, swallowing. It was oddly satisfying, and something curled up warm and happy in my stomach.

My nose filled with the smell of hot soil and wet leaves. Lexi was gone. She had left me. The kitchen, the house, contained too many reminders of her- pictures on the fridge, her favorite mug dirty on the counter, her shoes sitting, waiting, in the tray next to the door. I wanted out, to scrabble at the door like a panicked dog left home alone too long. Instead I dried my hands with the dish towel hanging from the cupboard handle above the sink and made my silent way back to my room. I shut my door and buried my face into my pillow.

But it did not smell right. It did not smell like Lexi, like dirt and grass and wildflowers. It did not smell like her Wolf. The sound that finally crawled out of my throat to be smothered into the pillow was a sort of sob and scream and laugh all twisted together into a sharp and throat-scratching bark. I wanted my sister.

The ferocious anger between sisters is a shifty, treacherous thing. I was so angry at her, for cutting me out and for leaving. And I wanted nothing more than for her to come back, to open that bedroom door and whisper for me to come in. I would snuffle after my sister like a puppy, sneaking into her room at every opportunity to roll myself into her bed and press my face into her pillow. I could still smell her there, just a ghost of cut grass and wild rose now, but it was a ghost I could still chase after with the determined desperation of the abandoned.

And chase I did. I looked for every bit of a trail she might leave, making my way to the library after school "to do homework" I told my parents. But I was chasing, and hopefully not chasing my own tail. I dug through the internet for a hint of her —Lexi, Alex, Alexandra, every name she had tried on to see how it fit. Our internet time had never been monitored at home and I took advantage of having the liberty to sit and search. Somewhere there had to be a trace of her. She could not stop at shoes left sitting by the front door. But there was nothing I could find on social media, and I tried any I could create an account for. No photos, no videos, no updates, no signs of life. I tried both her emails, but it was nothing more than shouting into a wide darkness, met only with silence.

We moved in my last years of middle school, hauling boxes in the June sun alongside the small group of movers Dad had hired. I sat on the hastily made bed in my new room on the second floor of the new, bigger, house, the space a mess of boxes. A new space, somewhere my parents seemed to hope where we would not be haunted by the ghost of a missing child. The next few days were spent unpacking, organizing, settling in. Finding out where I fit in this new space and family dynamic.

And at night I made my wolf.

I had no one, no sister to describe him to, to explain him to. So I lay in bed, eyes almost closed and lights off, and whispered fervently. Mine was an older wolf, coarse grey coat and sharp green eyes. His breath was hot on my face, nose dry as he snuffled and learned me just as I learned him. As I discovered him. It was less a creating than a slow unfolding. One night I found my way to the cracks in the pads of his paws, the way they caught at the bedding, the slight scratch of their edges on the wood flooring as he paced around me. The next I reveled in the feel of powerful muscles bunching and releasing as he leapt from the floor to my side, the graceful lack of effort. My sister's wolf had been fascinating, interesting to a young outsider as I lay beside her on bed. My own wolf was beguiling.

He began to seep into the daylight hours. There was just too much of him to contain in the quiet bits of night before sleep. I was fidgety, needing to shift and move, trying to alleviate a tension and an itch I could not properly locate. I used to get restless legs when I was younger— this was restless legs over my entire body. It made it hard to sit still, to focus. I found myself pleading with my wolf one night, asking for help. He curled around me, fur perfectly coarse, and rested his head beside mine. His breath was warm, smelled just a bit like old dead things. Old meals, crushed grass, damp soil. My wolf. I closed my eyes and relaxed.

I wrapped myself in my wolf to ease the tension that plagued me. I gained a reputation as an airhead in school, drifting off with my wolf as he chased an interesting scent only to be started by a question directed at me during classes. My grades suffered and by the end of high school my parents were frustrated enough to sit me down and try to talk through things with me.

"Is there anything we can help with, honey?"

Sitting in the recliner, legs folded to the side and under, and my nose filled with the smell of soil in the sun, moldering leaves...

"Allie. Your father asked you a question."

There was something sharp in Mother's voice, a reprimand that rankled. I turned a wolf's unblinking stare her way, holding otherwise perfectly still, muscles relaxed and at the same time ready to spring in any direction.

"Answer your father, Allie."

I lifted my upper lip to show just a flash of teeth, a warning.

"I am not going to lose both of you." Mother's voice was hard, vicious, but my wolf could smell the panic on her and he settled that awareness around me like a cozy blanket. Mother was scared. Mother was scared and I was calm.

"Mother." The voice was rough, soft. I knew it was my voice, but I could hear that rumble of my Wolf there was well. "Mother, what happened to Lexi?"

"I am, we might as well."

Mom flinched, she looked at Dad with eyes gone wide, nostrils flared in startled betrayal. "Andrew..."

"One is gone already. How do you think ignoring it will help?" Calm, level-headed, but I could smell the acrid tang of unhappiness on him. Defeat was a sharp and bitter flavor. I rolled it around in my mouth, getting familiar with how it stung.

"Ignoring what?" I asked, voice still soft. Mom was the upset one, shifting her weight and digging her nails into her palms, and I directed the question at her. The scent of blood grabbed my attention as one nail cut a bit too deep. Just under my skin, my wolf held perfectly still, at attention, waiting.

"On your head be it." Mom snarled, and I could almost see the wolf that ghosted along behind her, a skeletal and miserable wisp of a thing, forgotten and neglected. I balanced on the line between wanting to weep and wanting to snarl. That poor wolf...

It vanished like so many pieces of dust in disturbed air catching the sunlight as mom stood, grabbing her phone from the coffee table in a quick, sharp movement as she stalked from the room. Tail between her legs. Scared. Alone.

"Dad?" It was more my voice now, the question pulling the word up at the end, pulling it out of the quiet rumble of my wolf.

"One second. Let me get something." He stood with a creak, his expression almost grim. "Be right back."

He went upstairs to the master bedroom. I tracked him by every creak in the floor and soft sound of things being shifted gently around. It took him a couple of minutes, and his steps were slower, dragging through thick reluctance, as he returned to the living room where he handed me something silently.

It was an old, slim book. It smelled of dust and dirt and countless dirty hands. I looked up at him, head tilted just slightly to the side.

"It's from your mother's family. A record, of sorts. Probably an explanation." He scratched the back of his head, looking both uncertain and uncomfortable. And tired. Very tired. "We had thought, maybe…" He looked up then, met my eyes as bold as any wolf. "We had thought that maybe it would miss us. Miss you. It doesn't hit every generation, after all."

"What doesn't?"

"The madness." The words were quiet, as if saying them too loud would give them more reality, more life, than father was willing.

I flipped open the book, sniffing away a sneeze. It was a handwritten record, the first pages, the oldest, being in handwriting so outdated I could hardly make out the words. As I turned pages, the shape of the things written there became more familiar. Names, it was a catalog of names and dates. Some of them I recognized from my time working with my Ancestry account. They were relatives long gone who had gone missing. I returned my attention to my father. "The madness?"

"The wolf." There was something in my father's voice, something heavy and unhappy, thick with distrust and distaste. It hung between us for a heartbeat like a threat.

My wolf came to full life then, teeth bared and overwhelming me. A ghost caught out in the open, and gone on the offensive. My father fell back in terror as my wolf lunged towards him, a deep snarl and the shatter of the glass of water that had been on the end table the only sounds.

My father.

My wolf wanted blood and violence, to defend itself.

My father.

I howled, the sound that of an upset human rather than the resonant call of a wolf. I bit my cheek, drawing blood. I sat myself back onto my recliner, panting. It was a game I had played with my sister, listening to her telling me stories about her wolf. She left me, and I continued to lay awake at night and dream of wolves. My wolf. I nurtured my wolf, grew him into something beautiful and fierce and the whole time wanted nothing more than to find my sister so I could tell her stories, her head pillowed on my chest. I had not wanted to hurt my father, who cowered there where he had fallen back, fallen to the floor. His eyes were wide and horrified.

My wolf was restless, pacing inside me, and I needed to move. I needed to leave that room and the scent of my father's terror before something worse than a broken glass happened.

I wanted to go home.

I had never considered going back to the house I had been born in, the little rural ranch that I had crept through to visit with my sister in her bedroom each night. It had been a handful of years since I had last been in that house, and it looked it had been a long time since anything human had walked down the hall from kitchen to bedrooms. The windows had been boarded up, my mother's roses left to go wild, but the front door was open, vandalized. I walked inside, so much bigger then I had left, so much more. The small area rug just inside the door was green with growing things and broke apart under my feet. With the door left open, the world had crept into that small house. It was exposed, damaged. I felt sympathy for the structure.

A childhood game. That is all it had been. Listening to my sister tell me stories about a Wolf before bed. My head hurt with the effort of standing and staying, of being me. Just a game. But it spoke to something deep in us, a ghost that haunted our family and no one ever spoke about because it was impossible and horrible.

I would argue the horrible, even as I stood there in the remains of that broken old house, the place I had been born and had been young with Lexi, staring at the floor I only just remembered. The need to move stung every muscle and I quivered in place, panting. It was not horrible. The way I moved was grotesque, muscles stuck between where I held them and where they wanted to be. It hurt, oh did it hurt, and the smell of dirt and grass and wildflowers filled my nose so sharply my eyes watered and then it was gone. But it was not horrible, my wolf.

He sang to me, my wolf. A deep crooning and loving song. How many of my missing relatives had stood this way, in childhood homes, and listened? How many had staggered from their lives trying to soothe a need that would not let them rest?

How many children had lay in bed and dreamed of wolves?

I lifted my head when I heard her, smelled her, a trace of rose dancing through the heavy soil and dust smells of this place. Hers was a lean and long-limbed wolf, cautious as it stalked towards me through the open door, ears back and shoulders down, a dark wolf with the same bright eyes I remembered from that stolen glance years and years ago. I dropped to my knees onto the dirty floor, hands pressed in dirt and the carapaces of insects long dead. My stomach roiled, but I kept my eyes on my sister's wolf. On my sister.

"Lexi." My voice was thick, the name hard to shape. My mouth was all wrong, tongue moved in unfamiliar ways, against unfamiliar and uneven teeth. My gums hurt. Everything hurt.

Everything but the brush of my sister against my side. Her fur was coarse but that sensation, that contact, pulled my eyes closed in pure bliss, allowed something in me to relax.

I described my Wolf to my sister, my eyes pressed tight and my voice thick and slow and painful. But I told her about the cracked pads of his feet, the strength in his muscles, his sharp green eyes and thick grey coat. I had wanted to tell her for so long. I had wanted to breathe in the dirt and grass and flower scent of her, of her wolf, and to tell her about mine.

My sister. I had found my sister.

I finally let myself relax, let my words run dry. Stopped looking, chasing. Stopped hunting.

My wolf sneezed, the dust of the old human den tickling his nose. The other wolf looked at him with laughing gold eyes. My wolf raised a lip, baring just a hint of teeth, then gave a slow wag of the tail.

It was comfortable, being my wolf. I stretched, exulting in the feeling of the pull of muscle, at the way everything seemed to be right, finally. The edge and need that had nipped at my heels for so long was gone. I had wolf and sister. I had one brief thought of my mother, of the way she had howled that she was losing both her daughters, but wolf savaged the memory until it was destroyed. This was me. The real and whole me. Tooth and claw and freedom.

Lexi nosed at me, a question. She had been running free for so many years. I was grateful she had come back for me. I was so happy she had come back for me. I nipped at her playfully, and was immediately distracted by the shape and strength of that deadly jaw. Lexi bumped her shoulder to mine, getting my attention. Her movement and gestures were a language I was just learning, acting on the instinct of my wolf. Excited I danced in place and then howled. I poured Allie into that howl, wishing her well, letting mother know I would be alright.

Two wolves ran out into the night, leaving the old house behind.

LIKE SAND IN YOUR TEETH

The first time I saw her I laughed. There is nothing elegant about hiking pants up past knees in order to scrabble around in the sand and surf. Her skin was browned, legs obviously used to being exposed to the sun. The look of concentration on her face, furrowed forehead and intent eyes all crinkled at the corners, was endearing enough that I did not continue to snicker. She would not have heard me anyway. The barking laugh of a seal is not so loud when compared to the shouting and slamming of the surf. I floated out past the break of the waves, head just above water, and watched as she scavenged for things I could not fathom. There was no food to be found where she searched and scrounged, no treasure I could remember being buried. I had no idea what she could possibly be doing, bouncing around the shore like a willet.

I have always been cursed with far more than my share of curiosity. I rode a wave in, slipping out of my skin after being deposited gently on shore and stood, hands crossed behind my back in an imitation of posture I had observed over the years, and leaned close. "What are you looking for?"

I am glad I did not startle the girl's heart into stopping

permanently. I did give her a bit of a fright, stepping up to look over her shoulder without any prior announcement of my presence. I suppose I scandalized her, at least a little. After she recovered from her gasp and clumsy leap to the side her eyebrows drew tight over her forehead as she regarded me.

"Who are you? What are you doing? Where…" she gestured at me, a flush rising to her cheeks to color them as if they had been kissed by the sun.

"I couldn't very well swim in my clothing, now could I? I left it on the beach." It was not a lie—my sealskin was settled neatly between some stones a few paces down the shore, where the wave had set me. Our concepts of clothing may have differed, but that was hardly the point of her inquiry. "My name is Coira. What are you looking for? Can I help?"

She frowned, ever so slightly, but her stiff and startled posture eased. "I am looking for shells."

Shells. Of all the little, silly things in the sea. Of all the things I loved best. Of course she was looking for shells. She had a few settled in a piece of cloth she held out for me to see. Some colorful, some bearing the marks of rough treatment, all meticulously selected as no two were the same. This was a fair place for shells, the tide left some behind when it retreated, and the shore was long here. She knew this place, and her task, well.

"I am Kyla." She offered me her name with the same stoic dignity with which she chose to ignore my nudity. "I suppose you could help, but I need to be home soon."

"I am very good at finding shells." I smiled, but stopped short of showing teeth. No need to scare her off, not when she was proving to be so interesting.

It was enjoyable, mucking around in the sand, skipping past waves as they came pounding down around us, hauling the tide in as time passed. Kyla relaxed a bit as we worked. I took credit for that, as I am more than a fair singer and added my own tune to the symphony of wind and wave and gull as her shell collection grew.

The tide was fully in when Kyla drew back from the water, let her pants down in relatively dry safety, and tilted her head as she regarded me. Her eyes were very green, like the eel grass that danced sinuously with the current. "I am going to go home now."

"I should as well."

I will never tire of it, the way shock twists and tickles through human expressions. I most likely should have been borne a Pwca—I took far too much delight in the way Kyla gasped, almost dropping her shells, as I retrieved my sealskin, wrapped it about myself, and slipped back into the sea.

* * *

I DID NOT EXPECT to see her again the following day, walking that same bit of shoreline as if the tide had left her there. And the day after. I watched from just beyond the breaking waves, safe in my skin. It was one thing to tease and taunt a human, quite another to appear after revealing my nature. I have seen too many of my sisters taken as seal wives—their skins snatched and hidden, binding them to the shore as they slowly pined. I had no desire to partake of their unsavory fate.

"Coira?"

She called my name every now and then; the wind carried it to my ear as I watched her. It was unsettling, and I dove down deep in response, where the wind and her voice could not reach me.

But I always came back. Just as drawn to that bit of shoreline as she apparently was. Drawn to the shoreline and the girl, and then young woman, who walked along it. I don't know how long we played this game of staying just out of reach, she and I —time is strange to those of us who have no use for aging. One day I noticed she was taller, broader in the hips and wider in the chest—no longer my little shell-waif, and lovely.

And not alone. I did not like the fact she brought a male with her to our beach. It felt like a breach of some unspoken contract.

I suppose I should not have chosen to ignore her for as long as I had, granting only a flash of my spotted skin, or splash of my departure. I could not blame her, but I did.

I came out of the surf and arranged myself atop the rocks where I liked to set my sealskin, sprawled so that the sun caught the pale skin of my long legs, of back and breast. And I smiled. I smiled the way Seal Maidens do when they want to lure a lover into the surf. To hold and kiss as they sank deep. A smile filled with the knowledge only one of us would return to the surface. I wanted him gone, wanted his hair to tangle with the plants on the deep sea bed as they danced. He saw me. How could he not? And he started to come to me. It was how this scene always played out. I raised a hand, beckoning.

"Coira?" Her voice ruined it. Something inevitable and too similar to shame churned in me where vengeful anticipation had been. I bared my teeth, showing every sharp edge my enticing smile had concealed. They cut through glamour as well as flesh and he stumbled back, face a tangle of confusion and fear.

I just wanted him off my shore. I wanted her off my shore, if it was no longer to be a thing we shared between us. Selkie Lords control the storms, selkie maids are a beauty cold and cruel when we creep out from behind our magic of diversion and distraction. She had been an interest, nothing more. Nothing more to me than an oddity with which to pass the time.

"Coira…please. This is my brother Benneit. I wanted him to see you, to meet you." Kyla's voice grew quiet. "To see why I come here day after day."

"Why do you?" My voice was hard as old, dead coral, tone just as sharp. I had my sealskin secure in one fist, should I need —no, want—to leave.

"To see you. I keep hoping you will come ashore to look for shells with me. To walk with me." Her voice was soft, uncertain, nothing like the blunt child I had been so enamored of. But it curled through my fury, warming my desire to remain hard and cold.

"We are fickle, those who are fey. You should not wait on us."

"But she did." Benneit interrupted, with a voice rough as the tides, but so quiet.

My hand convulsed around my sealskin, reflexively making sure it was still there. Human male. Thief. Prey. Kyla's kin. Too many different impressions all fighting for my attention. I flashed my teeth again, covering my confusion with ferocity. "I did not ask her to."

"You did not send her away."

I did not like this, did not like him. He stirred up the waters until they were too murky to make sense of. I did not like having to take note of my own emotions. I was better made to shift with the moon's pull, drift with the tides and take the storms as they came. Introspection does not come naturally to a selkie.

Of course I did not send her away. She interested me. The soft song of her voice, the way she lifted her pants and stepped just so as she moved across the beach, the play of her hair in strong coastal winds across her back—these things caught my attention. Held it. I did not want her to go away, to turn her bright eyes elsewhere. "I want her here." It was an unwelcome admission, one that made me vulnerable. I did not want to be vulnerable, especially in front of Benneit. I started to pull my sealskin over me, covering as if I were cold.

"I do not want you, your skin, selkie." Benneit held out a staying hand, stood very close to Kyla a moment to whisper words that the wind failed to carry to my ears, and then slowly began to walk away.

"Coira, may I come sit with you?"

Backwards, backwards. This was all backwards. I should not be the one nodding slowly, as if enthralled, and watching every step she took to get to my side. I should not notice how the muscles in her calves worked with every step though wet sand, the way her toes flattened and grasped for purchase. I should not notice how her breathing had sped up, just a bit, should not be imagining how her heartbeat would sound close to my ear.

I should not be dreaming of the touch of her skin, the patches that promised to be warm as they were a sun-touched red.

She should be dreaming of me.

Perhaps she had been. She lowered herself to sit with a delicacy that spoke of discomfort, nervousness. I could clearly see the way her pulse pressed against the skin of her throat now that she was beside me. I wanted to run sharp teeth along that stretch of skin, feel her pulse quicken.

Instinct can be hard to manage, especially when the warm human smells of sweat, grass and dirt tickled at me with every breath. She gasped slightly, delightfully, as I nipped at her neck, ran my cheek along the curve of her chin. She tasted of things I had no name for—I only knew they fascinated and excited me. So different than the sea.

"Coira?" Her voice was a vibration against my cheek as I pressed it against hers. There was a note, the way she turned my name up at the end with inquiry, that pleased me.

"Hello," I murmured, touching her for the first time, greeting her as I had not before. "Hello, Kyla."

I wanted to touch her, taste her, keep her. But I did not want to drag her into the depths, wrapped in my embrace, did not want to steal her last breath or dine on her flesh. Possessive, yes, but not in a way I had wanted to possess a human before. I rolled the realization around in my mouth, getting a sense of the sandy grit of it, trying to get the taste of it, the taste of her. I pulled back from her. "What do you want?"

"What?"

"What do you want? Why do you come here, reliably as the tides? Why do you risk bringing your kin to me?"

"I wanted to see you again. I want to see you again." She was not struggling against me, even with my sharp angles and sharp teeth visible, so close. Her earnest desire tasted sweet, mixed well with the new sort of possessiveness causing my mouth to wet and anticipation to dance down my spine.

"I am here." She did not fear me. It pulled my mouth into a wide smile. "I gathered treasure for you." I pulled her to her feet, my sealskin falling forgotten from my lap to lay atop the rocks we had been sitting on. "Come. Come with me."

Those were not words uttered by a selkie that humans generally survive. But she came with me without hesitation, curiosity instead of trepidation in her eyes.

I set a fierce pace and we ran down the beach, leaving behind widely spaced tracks for the waves to sweep out of existence. We startled some gulls as I pulled her up to the small cave I had found years ago, splashing in and out during high tide, slipping in dry during low. The tide was coming high now and there was no avoiding dampening her pants as I coaxed her to duck through the low entrance.

The rocky shoreline held many such secret places close—this was the first I had shared. It was not a large cave, but we could stand without brushing against the ceiling. It was not deep enough to swallow its contents in gloom, and I could step back enough to watch Kyla take it in. She brushed a finger against the ancient barnacle shells on her left, wriggled her toes in a patch of optimistic sea vegetation, and then pulled both hands to her face with a gasp as she looked forward.

Shells. I had been gathering them for her through the years, pulled from the deep places where they rested quietly, unbattered by the surf. I had polished fan muscles until they gleamed, piled periwinkles, constructed a collection of whelks beside a stack of cockles. All for the girl who had been collecting what the sea left behind.

Kyla turned towards me, eyes wide. "Coira...?"

"For you. It was always for you."

Her lips were rough as she leaned in, textured in a way that was new to me—dried out by sun and wind. They tasted ever so slightly of salt, just before they parted and her tongue touched mine. Then she tasted like nothing I had ever experienced before. And was warm, so very warm. Everything about the lithe human was warm. It had pulled the chill from my bones, from my magic, years ago. And I was just noticing.

I HAD EXPECTED her to take shells home with her, and she did—but it was such a select few. I could not understand her fascination with leaving the bulk of them in the cave, but I was pleased as she puttered about in the salty dimness, holding a shielded lantern up to this and that, to examine them better without moving them out into the sun. I offered to help her carry them, as I assumed there were simply too many for her to move alone.

She rounded on me, fierce as I had never seen her. "No. These are ours. They stay here." And so they did, rearranged and settled to meet Kyla's mysterious standards.

She kissed me before she left that evening, eyes soft and warm with something not quite gratitude. Something far more tangled, entangling. I brushed a hand through her long hair, breathing deeply to catch as much of her as I could before she was gone. I was not content with our parting, wanting her to come with me. Wanting to follow her. But her death lay in my embrace in the sea, and mine would follow me up that shoreline unless I surrendered my sealskin.

My sealskin.

I raced back to the rocks by the surf where my skin lay crumpled but unfound. My magic and my freedom. I could not give it to her. I would make a feral, terrible seal wife.

I wrapped it tight around me, slipped back into the sea and down deep. To chase tiny silver fish through long branching vegetation and skeletal coral. To clear my mind.

My family waited, flashes of speckled sealskin through the forest of lazily waving sea vegetation. I tried not to meet their eyes, eyes that had gone hard with disgust and distrust. My brothers bumped against me, accusing. My sisters slid across my skin, trying to wipe the scent of the shore and of Kyla off of me. I was unfamiliar, inappropriate. Humans were for liaisons, languid slips into the deep. They were not to be returned to.

Accusations are thick to swim through, so I turned from my family and slipped off into the dark waters.

I was already remembering how Kyla tasted. The scent of her.

* * *

HER VOICE CALLED me up each day, summoning me from wherever the sea had taken me the night before. I always came ashore a woman, and slipped my sealskin some place safe when I felt safe she was not looking. It was not that I was afraid she would steal it, bind me. Not Kyla. Each day I hid it to fend off a twisty desire to hand it to her and let her pull me to her home.

I learned the curve of her neck, the little sounds she made when surprised and especially pleased. I traced the back of her knees, learning that was ticklish and enjoying how she twisted like a caught fish when I touched her there. I learned earlobes were for biting, ever so gently, for teasing. I learned that she was warm in every way I could make the word be. Her eyes were deep with it, her voice rich with it, her body infused with it. And I craved it. Craved her. I needed to hear her stutter out my name while her hands gripped me, needed to hear her laugh, sing. They said the selkies were the dangerous ones—Kyla's warmth was far more treacherous.

I ignored my family where they floated just past the break of the waves, as they sunned on quiet beaches or dove to hunt and play. I was not interested in sitting with my sisters and brushing my hair out in the moonlight, beckoning to humans clumsy enough to stumble upon our secret places. I pulled no mortal victims down with me, beneath the waves. I was a selkie tamed, and I was doing my best to ignore that fact.

"Benneit is off to sea."

We were laying on our backs on the beach, letting the morning sun dry the sweat from our skin. I was casting sideways glances, every now and then, proud of the sharp little marks I had left along her throat. Wondering what her family would think of them.

"Oh?" I rolled over, pillowed my head on her breast to better listen to the beat of her heart, noting it was quick, unsteady, and not from my attentions.

"He left with some other men from the village. They are going to work the fish run." Her hand raised to draw fingers through my hair, rub against my scalp. "I always worry when he is at sea."

"I am of the sea—and I would not harm him. He will return to you, safe and smiling." Her fingers were brushing across my forehead, soothing and distracting. Beneath my ear her heart had slowed a bit, but I could still taste her unease in the air. I wanted her happy, my warm human.

I pulled myself up and over Kyla, pressed my nose to hers before nipping at it lightly. "I will watch over him." I kissed her, all tooth and tongue and pressure. I set my promise deep into her, marking her to show my sincerity, caressing her to express affection and something uncomfortably close to love. She pressed back, taking what I offered, acknowledging what I didn't say while returning the emotion. We broke patterns and rules, my Kyla and I. We disrupted the established order of things just as soundly as we disturbed the sand beneath us.

She gave me a necklace before she left, as the sun was creeping towards the horizon. Carefully strung together, bits of shell and stone. She slipped it over my head and I smiled before curling my sealskin close. I stayed for a moment, not slipping back into the sea as swiftly as I had in the past. Kyla knelt down close and ran a hand across my head, brushed against the jewelry still secure around my seal-form's neck. Nothing was said, but I could taste 'goodbye', harsh as I inhaled.

I nudged against her, once, and then slipped into the surf, following the sloping sand out until I could dive deep.

* * *

I KNEW next to nothing about ships and sailing, but fish runs were familiar. I followed warm currents and flashes of scale until I met up with sprawling schools of fish darting and feeding. Breaking the surface with a huff I glanced about, seeking any shape or motion that was not sea life or wave.

There, past a pair of resting pelicans a small group of boats bobbed atop the water. I could just make out bits of speech, the splashes of their work. There I would find Benneit. I startled the pelicans with a happy little bark before starting to swim

The sea was thick with my family as I grew close to the working ships. They filled the sea with their displeasure, disgust, until even the fish sensed it and started to flee. An elder brother hit me as I swam, the impact of his larger body against mine knocking me to the side, hurting.

'Why?' Pleading, confused.

'You are of the sea.' It was a snarl, a shout, and my family battered me with their bodies and their magic, keeping me from the kin of my beloved Kyla.

I felt it rising, the storm that was my brothers' fury. I felt the magic seethe up from the depths, pulling unpredictable currents and impossible waves in its wake. I could sense it spiraling through the sky, stringing together clouds. I struggled against my family as I felt the storm break all around me.

The creak and moan of ships breaking apart filled my ears, and I was not sure who my family was punishing—their errant daughter or the human that had tamed me.

They left me to flounder and recover in the storm—humans had been thrown to the sea, their point had been made. Not a sympathetic eye was to be found amidst my siblings, cousins, not a friendly brush of fin or head. I was left to pull myself together as best I could, and to follow like a good daughter. A good selkie.

I pulled myself together, and swam towards the wreckage.

Never had I directly opposed my family so. Alone amongst the storm that was a Selkie Lord's fury I dove again and again, trying to find Benneit amidst the seething and unsettled water. The sea was still my mother, no matter how I neglected Her, and I wriggled as well as I could through crest and froth, making progress where things not fey would surely be swamped. A bit of red caught my eye—Benneit's fox hair limp against his face as he clung desperately to a small bit of board, all that remained of the ship I had felt, heard, splinter and start to sink.

He was so pale, so cold, and barely breathing. I was not in much better shape. I had no way of pulling him to shore—there was not enough strength left to me. My family had made sure of that. I was not sure he would have had the capacity to cling to a seal even if I had the strength to ferry him to safety.

Kyla loved him so.

It seemed I was going to give her my sealskin to keep after all. I removed it, gasping briefly at the sensation of arms and legs in the angry waters, missing webbing and insulating fur. The world was a jumble of missing sensations and perceptions, but I could not linger on disorientation. I had to be quick, swimming like this was not natural, not easy. I curled my sealskin around Benneit's cold, still form, wrapping him in magic freely given. A seal slipped awkwardly off the bit of wood he had been clinging to and stared at me with wide dark eyes. I wanted to laugh, tried to, but choked on water as a wave hit me in the face. I scrabbled onto the wood Benneit had so recently abandoned. So strange—fingers and toes and skin in the ocean. I hated the feel of water in my ears, how very cold I was becoming. I hated feeling helpless. I could not wrap my head around being in danger from the sea.

Selkie-Benneit nudged me with his nose, eyes a mix of concern and confusion. "It's okay." I coughed to try and clear water out of places I did not think it had any business being. "Be safe. Go home. Go to Kyla."

It was very cold in the ocean without a sealskin. And I was very tired. My Mother wanted her wayward daughter—and she could have her. At that moment I was too worn to be rebellious, too mortal. I thought of Kyla's warm eyes as I closed my own.

* * *

I DID NOT EXPECT to wake up, but when I did it was with a choking cough that turned inappropriately quickly into a rough laugh. Kyla was asleep beside me, head pillowed on her arms as she rested up against the bed.

Bed. Dry and warm and still. This was very new, and I was still too raw to sort out whether or not I was interested and excited about new sensations.

"Coira?"

My waking, barking laugh, and slight shift had woken Kyla, and she rubbed at her eyes as she spoke my name.

I suppose I was still Coira, but the name curled differently through my ears now, carried a different meaning. Coira the girl. Coira without magic to let her sink beneath the sea as safely as a babe curling into its mothers arms. There was no more Coira the selkie. The realization, in the quiet that follows decisions made amidst conflict and confusion, was like sand in my teeth. Abrasive, bitter—I could not work through each individual granule, they were all too adept at getting into and under my skin.

I could still taste the grit of the ocean in my mouth, and for once the ocean was Other, external. I was no longer of the sea; the tides did not sing through my blood with each pulse of my heart.

"Hey, Coira. Talk to me." Kyla wrapped her arms around me as if trying to hold me together, hold me in. "Benneit brought you. He told me."

She smelled the same, dirt and dust and human sweat, a hint of something fresh from the oven. Her voice was warm, heavy with concern and something close to that human entanglement known as love.

She was my selkie maid, beckoning me to come to her, to turn from everything I knew. I had been beaten at my own game. She was warm, and pressed tight against me so I could feel her breath, hear the rhythm of her heart and the tides of the body that it ruled.

"Thank you, Coira. Thank you for my brother."

That was not what I wanted to be thanked for, all things considered. I wanted to be thanked for not-so-soft kisses and little piles of gathered treasure. I wanted to be thanked for crooked smiles and runs across the beaches laughing in the moonlight. I did not want to be thanked for being human.

"Will you stay?"

"Yes." My voice was rough, all of its pleasantness burned away by the ocean. Of course I would stay. How could I not? I had been mesmerized by this woman since she showed me a handful of sea shells, so long ago.

We would learn secrets, Benneit and I. He would learn just what hid down in the darkest parts of the ocean, would learn how a seal laughed and how it felt to coax a pretty lass out into the waves. I would learn how Kyla looked as she pulled bread from the oven, how dirt felt beneath my feet and what grass smelled like when it was rolled in. I would learn what to do with that burning abrasive emotion known as love, to become familiar with the way it felt like I had a mouthful of sand the first time I tried to shape the word with my voice.

"I will stay."

Author's Note: "Like Sand in Your Teeth" was originally published, in a different form, in 2018. This is the story as it was originally written and meant to be.

OBLIGATIONS

I would have never found this place if Bear had not been walking with me. She caught my attention with a huff that stirred up old leaves, the dry scent of secrets and decay. An oak leaf, brown with tips curled in as if it was starting to make a fist was caught in her ghost of a breath and landed delicately in a bit of still water.

Bear's breath was warm in my back as I walked to the waters edge. They weren't visible if you looked directly at them, but I had been warned about that. From the corner of my eye I caught a glimpse of the stepping stones. Once I knew they were there, and convinced myself to trust that they would stay there, I was able to step onto the first bit of worn granite. Then the second. Foot after careful foot until I was in the center of the mountain lake. A densely forested island rose before me, water pressing up against its rocky shore. A handful of little brown birds gossiped as they foraged in nearby bushes.

I leaned back, just a little, allowing the warmth of Bear to comfort me as I waited. Bear swatted absently at some fish swimming around her in the shallow water.

I did not know this place, but it knew me. My family, at least.

It knew Bear. Ma had come here every autumn for as long as I could remember, and her mother before her, Bear along side, guiding. With Ma gone now, faded away with the last of the sunflowers this summer, I made the trip.

I did not have to wait long. The sun started to dip, reflecting off of the water and casting the tree tops in a glorious golden glow and a figure emerged from the trees. It seemed to unfurl into all the space being out of the thick undergrowth allowed, stretching up towards the dying sunlight like a spindly seedling. Brown and thin, a stick bug's build with a preying mantis' precise movements, it stood on the rocky shore across the last bit of restless water, facing me.

I wanted to assign it human qualities like hair and hand but it was a puzzle of stick and lichen. It's eyes were large and round and reminded me of eyes I had seen on dragonflies when I had been lucky enough to get close enough to examine them. It's quick jerky movements also reminded me of a dragonfly as it tilted its head, as it stared unblinking.

"You are not the right one."

I sighed, and Bear rumbled a bit of reassurance. It's not like I had thought they would not notice. But I had hoped. "Enid is unavailable." There were layers to that explanation, and each one of them bit.

"You are second."

I was the second born, yes, but I was all they were going to get. "I am Siobhan. Sister of Enid. Daughter of Moira. I am here to fulfill our obligation to the Queen."

"Where is your sister?"

"My sister chooses to neglect her obligation. I am here in her place."

It's bright eyes blinked once, and then it nodded, a jerk of its narrow head. "I accept. As the Queen accepts. For this cycle. I am Keeper, the Rememberer for the Queen. You may come across to us."

Reassuring myself with a pat to the backpack I had carried in with me on this hike and a quick press of my face against Bear, I stepped from my rock to the shore. It was like receiving a jolt of electricity, making my hair stand on end and a shiver to stumble down my spine. The ground seemed unwilling to receive me, making its displeasure known as it roiled and grumbled beneath my feet, sending waves up and over the stepping stones behind me. The air tasted wrong and my lungs heaved and wheezed as they tried to get their bearings. It was the light that caught me the most, the way it seemed to break into colors that were too bright and sharp around the edges. It revealed things in the shadows my attention danced away from in self defense.

All around me the bushes seemed to be hiding whispers in the rustling of leaves as they shifted branches aside, providing me an easy path to follow as Keeper began to walk away from the shore. Keeper didn't seem to care if I followed and I had to shake off the shock of being somewhere that didn't make any sense, ignoring the movement and whispers and the way the air seemed reluctant to fill my lungs.

These were things that had been told to Enid. She had been taught what to do and how to do it, Mom's quiet voice always so patient. I had listened, of course. So I knew some of it at least. I knew to follow Keeper to the clearing surrounded by honeysuckle and rose, to come to the middle but no further. To wait as it paused just a few feet away. I knew to wait for the Queen to take notice.

I felt it, the shift in the air, a sharp bit of frost that wilted some of the flowers around the edge of the clearing. It was the signal Keeper had been waiting for. We had the attention of the Queen. It look at me with those dragonfly eyes, the insect mandible of its mouth clicking impatiently.

"I am Siobhan, daughter of Moira. I have come with our rent." I was proud that my voice only cracked a little. Had it been Enid here she would have recited out matrilineal line, back to the savvy old witch who had made the first agreement with the Queen of this place. I did not know their names, and I felt less for it.

I fumbled with my backpack, snagging the zipper twice as I tried to get it open after hauling it off of my shoulder. I removed two jars of carefully canned apple butter sweetened with maple syrup and honey, a large unlabeled jar that held Mom's apple moonshine, and three apples fresh from their climate controlled storage. They gleamed in the light of this strange place.

Keeper examined my offering, tilting his head to each side, mandibles clicking. Then it nodded. "The rent is paid, and recorded."

The bitter edge of winter swept through the clearing, bringing with it waves of magic that made my head hurt and stomach roil. And this was the Queen's approval, traced in hoarfrost.

"Siobhan, daughter of Moira, you may leave, and not return. We would see Our tenant proper next cycle. As was agreed." The Queen's voice was honey and ice, sharp and beautiful. I did not see her—I did not look towards the edge of the clearing, into the chill wind.

"Yes, my Queen." I bowed, the best I could dressed as I was for a hike and not Court. Keeper did not seem inclined to see me back, and I was keen on spending as little time in the Queen's overwhelming presence as possible, so I felt for Bear's warm, solid presence. I am a second daughter, and magic did not come easily for me, but I fumbled my way back down the shifty path, through the rustling and murmuring that tried to lead me astray until I reached the shore and could see Bear waiting for me in the water.

She wasn't even mine, that old ghost of a sow, but I leaned into her with relief as I stepped off the island and out of the worst of the chill of the Faerie Queen's displeasure. The rent was accepted. My family was safe under the queen's favor. But I was not welcome here again. Even now I could feel eyes on me. Bear rumbled a warning that sent ripples through the water and I started the careful walk across the stones and back to the shore I had started on.

Bear trailed me, watching my back. She wasn't mine, but she had been my mothers, shaped out of loss and sorrow when she had found a young sow dead on the side of a rambling mountain road. Bear belonged to Enid now, but she kept the necklace of bone and claw in a drawer, neglected. Bear kept me company, and showed me the ways Enid was disinterested in walking.

I would never have found the way home if Bear had not been walking with me, gently nosing me when I started off in the wrong direction through rock and fern and hemlock. We paused so Bear could rub her back on a massive hemlock. We startled some turkeys, one hen running herd on a rambling group of adolescents. The woods were a bit fae, close as they were to a proper Queen and Court, and I was glad for Bear's presence even as we came through the dense sugar bush that lined our orchards. Bear huffed, bumped her head against me, and turned back into the woods.

She was not mine, and I could not ask her to accompany me any further.

I did not need her as I walked down a row of Gala apples. I knew the orchards. I had been tending them since I was old enough to be trusted with pruning tools. I knew water shoot from branch, the insidious hint of rust, the dense clumps of clinging aphids. I knew how to look after our trees. Mom had raised us in them, on them. She taught us the quiet songs that she had learned from her mother. Songs to support new trees, to encourage those in their prime, and the quiet songs of thanks to the trees entering the end of their life. The orchard welcomed me back and I ran mental fingers through the web of the trees, check in, checking for disease or discomfort, Satisfied, I turned down the path that would take me back to the house. I would walk the orchard in the morning. Today I was tired.

The house was an old farmhouse that, in the way of farmhouses, had started to sprawl. Each generation of Greenspun witches, back to the first, hand added their own touch to the place. A bit of a maze of additions and confusion of color and style — and it was all mine. Enid was not in residence. She never was. I let myself in a front door that needed repainting, kicked off my shoes and made my way across worn hardwood floors to the kitchen.

I had met the Queen today. I deserved a nice cup of chamomile tea.

Then I would call Enid and give her the good/bad news.

I brewed my tea too strong. My mother would scowl. And I used tea bags instead of loose leaves or herbs, so I couldn't read what they wanted to tell me as they sprawled around the bottom of the cup. Grandmother would be appalled. But it was quick, it was easy, and having had a fortifying drink I had no excuse.

I used the house phone. This was Business, not pleasure.

"What now?" Enid sounded just as she always did, as if I had disturbed her from the most important or exciting thing in the world. I was an imposition, an inconvenience.

I sighed. "It's done for this year, Enid. But its on you next fall solstice. The Queen won't accept me again next year."

"I'm not interested."

"It's your duty." This was a worn out argument— the previous version having resulting in the trek I had made today. "Enid, you're the oldest. You have to do it."

"Screw it."

She hung up on me. I held the old phone for a moment longer, eyes closed. Enid had made it clear that she was disinclined to follow the family Work years ago. She moved out at eighteen. She didn't even come to moms memorial, just stopping by the house one afternoon for a box of heirlooms I had demanded she collect, because mom had wanted it that way. The green of our witchery glowed brightest in her, and she hated it. She wanted nothing more to do with me, with the beautiful quiet of the green things we tended and the promises we had made. It was just me now.

"Fuck."

What was I going to tell the Queen?

* * *

THE HARVEST WENT WELL— it always did. It was good to see so many of our regular helpers return again this year. The pay was good and I made sure they were looked after, offering them space in the sprawling old house that was far too big and far too quiet for just me. I fell into the rhythm of the harvest— greeting, cooking, directing. Crates got filled, crates were transported. Money came in, money went out, and the glorious busy of the season came to the same sudden end just as the season stretched into winter.

I left out a bowl of milk and honey, a loaf of fresh bread, and thanked the Queen and Court for their grace as soon as silence returned to the house. The orchard was a quiet and content hum as the trees settled for the colder season.

The cold was never too harsh. The summers were never too hot. We always had just enough rain The Queen looked after her tenants.

At Yule I went out into the trees, offering warm cider and banging pots and pans with the same abandon I had had since I was very young. I had always loved pushing through the snow to stand in the middle of a stand of sleepy Empire trees, and making a racket, waking them up, calling sap to start moving, trees to start stretching and thinking about the blooming season. Trees move slowly— they needed the reminder at Yule so that they would get things moving by spring.

I missed mom as I stood there in the snow, grateful for our sheltered space near the mountain lake, and banging a battered spoon into a cast iron pot and stretched myself throughout my favorite Empire trees, thanking them for their work and suggesting they start thinking about spring. Wasailing should never be lonely work.

Bear came to me, and while she couldn't join in my seasonal Work her presence, the ghost of her warmth, was welcome.

"Bear. Come in by the fire. Sit with me."

I did not think she would. I did not think she could. But Bear followed me back through the snow. I set my spoon, pan, and empty jug of mulled cider on the counter, surprised to turn around and see Bear sitting patiently just inside the front door. Waiting.

"Bear?"

She had always been at my mother's heels. She had lingered around the edges since Enid had left, and taken her bones. Bear yawned, and the sense of her stretched beyond the ghostly shape sitting there. It stretched through the house, settling in every shadow and dusty neglected corner. Oh. There. The sense of Bear was hot as fresh blood pooling in mother's room. I had not touched it. I didn't need it— I had my own space, there was so much space. But at Bear's urging I entered that room and, careful not to disturb anything else, reached under the bed until my fingers brushed something hard and cold and the sense of Bear filled me so strongly I sneezed. It was large, the bone I found, a leg bone. It was heavy and cracked— a souvenir of how Bear had died. I felt Bear fill me, a growling heavy strength and I spent time laying there reminding myself I was me, and reminding Bear that she was dead and she could not have me.

Ghosts were dangerous things, even ghosts as familiar as Bear. "I am sorry, Bear." And I was. I was sorry she was dead, and that mother had seen fit to shape a familiar ghost out of her. But that sympathy was not going to result in Bear having my warm flesh and blood to live in. Bear was mine now. The heat of her was present in a way she had never been before.

"You canny witch" I left mom the compliment as I left her room, bone in hand. She had given Enid the easy thing, the pretty thing, the comfortable totem that would bind her to Bear. But she had not given all the keys away.

Bear was lonely, that much I collected from the way she pulsed through me. Bear was lonely and frustrated and missed the little ones that used to play with her. Bear missed the Enid that had been. She had never gotten to know the Enid that was.

"Let's sit by the fire. It's Yule. No one should be alone."

* * *

THE QUIET OF winter was replaced by the bustle of orchard preparation and pruning. Spring came gently after a forgiving winter as we were spared the harsh storms and late frosts that plagued the areas around us. A glorious burst of spring blooms turned to setting fruit. I worked the rows, checking in with root, branch, leaf, and fruit. I had shadowed mom enough times that I new the routine, I knew the words, I knew the way to run my awareness through the trees as I greeted them.

I prepared the rent as the seasons started to turn and apples began to ripen. I followed Bear back up the mountain and to the edge of the still lake. She followed me back to the island where I stood and waited for Keeper to appear.

"Where is the tenant?"

I could see Keeper's faceted eyes gleaming out from the shadows on the edge of the island. They didn't blink.

"Enid, daughter of Moira, rejects her duties. I am here in her stead." I was proud that my voice didn't crack. It might have been the strength of Bear filling and supporting me.

More eyes, none of them friendly, gleamed into existence in the dark spaces all around the edge of the island. Bear growled a warning at whatever slithered through the water around our feet. I could just see an equine head thick with moss and muck and felt my stomach roil.

"I am Siobhan, daughter of Moira, of the line of the Greenspun witches. I do not know the words, I cannot recite the lineage. But I have come with the rent to fulfill our agreement."

"Unacceptable"

Winter descended upon the edge of the island, hoarfrost coating leaves and killing tender flowers. I could not look away from the Queen as she broke through the dying vegetation. She was beautiful, from the frost that glittered on pale skin to the winter-sky blue of her eyes. Her hair chimed with ice as it moved with her, and her every motion was sharp with danger. I dropped to my knees, ignoring the way my pants started soaking up lake water. I didn't want to collect any more details of the Queen's appearance lest they haunt me. Or tempt me. I could already feel a curl of lust trying to break through the chill of her presence. This was a Winter Queen, and winter was as deadly as it was beautiful.

"My Queen, please…" I started.

"No." The Queen's voice was sharp. "You are not the Greenspun Witch. You are not my tenant. You live and work on the grace and by the name of another. The contract is broken. The rent is not paid."

I looked up, panic surging through me. But the Queen was gone, and all of her Court had vanished with her. I knew better than to place one foot on that island uninvited. I turned to Bear, the weight of the rent in its pack on my back suddenly indescribably heavy.

"Bear. What do we do?"

Bear, of course, had no answer.

GENERATIONS OF GREENSPUN WITCHES had watched over this place, these orchards, through their covenant with the Queen. With that agreement shattered, time and the world caught up with our idyllic home. Autumn weather was sharper, more vicious. Winter was unpredictable and harsh. We lost trees that snapped in hard winds, that cracked under the weight of heavy wet snow. Frost cracks mangled trunks and frost heaves tore at the ground. I wandered the rows for Yule, spoon and pan and cider in hand, but the trees were silent, stressed. I went inside to sit by a Yule fire and wept. The world and its changes had caught up to us at last.

Spring brought the killing bite of late frosts and my depression turned to fury. My trees were hurting. I needed to have a conversation with my sister.

* * *

ENID LIVED in an old house that had been broken up into a number of apartments in the art district of Rochester New York. She shared space with other hopeful artists who had yet to hit whatever lucky break it was that would let them start to make any sort of sustainable income off of their work. I had dug the address out of a pile of old mail mom had left in a bin in the kitchen, written in mom's spidery handwriting. A letter sent to Enid and returned unopened.

Enid always did what Enid wanted. That had included ignoring the times mom asked her to come home and visit. Mom had not been healthy there at the end. It had been quick. Enid should have tried sooner. Tried at all.

I could feel the warmth of Enid's magic, even ignored and suppressed as it was, from my place on the front step. She would not know I was here— she did not pay attention to the green glow inside of her.

I should have knocked, but I was angry. The emotion had been a smolder for years, and the cries of my trees had fanned it, finally, into a roar. I told the door to open, so it did, the lock answering my request.

I was my mother's daughter, even if I was not the first. If Enid wanted to ignore and reject the mantle of her heritage I would take it up. I walked into the house, the warm seed of magic that I had been caring for all my life starting to set down strong roots and grow. Bear paced outside, a ghost of wind and warmth to any who might walk by, but I could feel her growl. It vibrated through my bones and came out through my mouth adding a strength and tenor and even a bit of temperance as I called my sister's name.

"Enid."

Names are special things. We recognize the shape of them, the taste of them, but we also notice the speaker, the particular way each mouth considers them and sets them free. Enid knew it was me. I rolled a lifetime of love and of loathing into the shape of those letters, let it all crash together in a name that dropped from my mouth to land with a sullen thud in the artificial quiet of the house. It scurried through the house, making its way upstairs to where a door opened.

My sister was vanilla and spice, a perfume and a personality. Sweet and sharp and sullen, it spread around her like a cloud as she came down the stairs, snapping my own name at me like a dart.

"Siobhan." She frowned, pausing a few steps shy of the first floor, keeping herself just a little higher than me. "Why are you here."

"You missed your appointment." I snapped out the words, teeth biting down hard around them. More than an accusation, it was a condemnation and I let her feel my displeasure.

"I didn't miss it. I wasn't coming to play with the fairies in the woods. You knew that." She paused, her lips curling into a mean little smile. "You here to cry about it?"

She could have been kind. She could have cared. She should have tried. But then, she wouldn't have been Enid.

"No." I had cried until my face was red and my nose thick with snot. I had curled up in bed alone in a big house and sobbed after the echoes of my sister that still haunted the place. I loved my sister, I always would, but I was done crying for her loss. "No." I was here to take something she had forfeited.

I called Bear to me, inviting her in. It was an easy thing. Of course my sister had neglected to Guard her own threshold. Another of Enid's neglected obligations, Bear was mine now, and I leaned into her strength as I worked.

It wasn't so different than gardening, tending magic. This was a different seed than I was used to working with, but I could still reach down into the dark quiet places of my sister, cup hands around roots, and pull the stunted seedling of her magic free. Enid didn't even know how to fight me, apart from reflexively trying to trap me there in the depths of her once she realized she could not keep me out.

But Bear, my Bear, was there to shoulder an opening for me, to hold it as I slipped free. I opened my eyes, full of the warmth of a magic that had become strong and whole.

Enid was hunched down, arms wrapped around her stomach. It must feel empty there now. I bared my teeth in something too feral to pass as a proper smile, unconsciously mimicking the curve of Bears lips around her teeth.

The great ghost of Bear paced and grumbled through Enid's home. But Enid was just a thin young woman who made art and enemies in her spare time who had no business sensing the passage of a restless spirit. She did shiver a bit in a mix of shock, having just had the warm core of her pulled free, and the slight chill breeze of Bear's movement.

"I hope you are happy." It was a truth, bright and honest as it flitted around the house like a hummingbird as soon as I shaped the sentiment. She wasn't, but I hoped she could be. Her magic was gone, would no longer drape itself through her art, would no longer be there to tug at the attention.

It was mine now, and I had Work to do.

"Goodbye, Enid."

I didn't wait for her response. I did not expect one.

I WOULD HAVE NEVER COME to this place if Bear had not walked beside me. Not in the autumn when the wind had bite, the days were short. Not when the Queen was so close to the height of her power. Even with the warmth and strength of Bear, this was a dangerous trip up the mountain.

There was ice reaching out from the edge of the water, creeping along bright and brittle leaves that collected in batches of deceptively warm color. The rocks were perilously slick, and my magic sang of danger in sharp brittle tones. I could not fall in. If I did, I was not coming back out. Even Bear traveled carefully from shore to shore this time, making sure to keep contact with my shadow. I shifted the bag on my back, adjusting my balance, and made that last little hop onto the shore.

"You trespass." Keepers voice buzzed and clicked with the memory of an insect cacophony, of the height of summer, but it had none of that warmth.

"I am here to see the Queen."

"Of course you are." Her voice slid under my skin and into my blood, icy and effervescent. Goosebumps prickled, my breath caught, and I wanted her like I had never wanted anything in my life. Even as her magic, so cold it burned, lit my nerves with a threat of frostbite I wanted more of it. Of her. But my magic rose and melted what it could. Bear huffed a warm breath across my neck and that was enough to thaw me out and deny the Queen a new toy. I pulled my spine straight and made myself meet eyes the sharp and lethal blue of a perfectly clear winter's day. I allowed myself to notice the points of the teeth in her flawless smile. And I dropped to a polite courtesy before speaking.

"I am Siobhan, daughter of Moira, of the line of the Greenspun witches. I do not know the words, I cannot recite the lineage. But I am the Greenspun Witch, and I have come to make an agreement. How much to rent this Land, as we have done in the past?

"Siobhan. Daughter of Moira." The Queen tasted the Names, tasted the magic contained in them. She licked her lips and smiled, every sharp tooth on clear display. "The Greenspun Witch. And you would like to renew the agreement? To pay the rent?"

I blinked, bowing my head for a moment to hide my surprise. No need to give away more than I had to. I had not expected it to be this easy. I had come hoping to be offered a new rental agreement, not a renewal of the one that had lapsed. "If it pleases you, my Queen."

"Black ice, hoarfrost, the sound of ice cracking in a silent morning, the song of a single snowflake. These are things that please me. With you, human witch, I will do business." She exhaled a Nor'easter and I focused very carefully on not shivering. "The rent will be one jar of maple syrup, the first of the season. A handful of marbles. A loaf of bread just burned enough to be honest. And three imperfect apples."

"The rent is recorded." Keeper intoned.

I did not realize, until Bear nudged my slightly, that it was my turn to speak, that something was expected of me. I did not know the words, but this was a familiar enough rhythm. The shape of deal making did not change overly much, even in this ancient company. "It is agreed." I made the words as firm as possible, clipped each syllable smartly enough to have made my mother proud.

The Queen smiled, and while the expression was no less feral this time around, there was something honestly affectionate in the expression. A kindly owner proud of and pleased with a hound that had learned an unexpected trick. "Until next year."

And she was gone, nothing left of her but a cold wind dragging its way down the spine, driving deep enough to chill bone, to startle the heart into give a sudden lurch before recovering and regaining its rhythm.

Keeper's mandibles worked and clicked and I think I was learning to read his alien expressions as his distaste and impatience were bold and obvious to me. I didn't want to see what happened if impatience shifted to anger. I gave another curtesy, the motion a bit thick and sluggish with cold, but still acceptable in form.

And then I turned my back on the Queen's home, her Court with its mutters and chitters and laughter, and I followed Bear home.

FOUR FOR BIRTH

"I bet you're too scared to do it."

It was spoken in the ritualistic way children skitter along the edges of proper bullying, folding pretense and posturing in with camaraderie until it became too much of a muddle to sort out and everyone just went along with it. The words seemed to bounce off of her like a lazy horsefly, leaving no visible damage and hardly any impression. She blinked, brushed at the bangs eternally falling into her eyes.

"Why do you even try with her? She's too slow and stupid."

Those words were familiar, the tang of them acidic as the chicken coop after a long winter. It brought a welling of tears to her eyes. Not slow, not stupid. Her tongue just got tangled so easily, words breaking free like startled birds instead of in well-formed sentences.

"I bet she doesn't even know who the witch is. C'mon, let's go."

She did too know the Witch. She gestured her understanding, but her classmates had already moved on, the group of young teens ranging along the road like a pack of stray dogs. She let her hands drop to her sides with a useless flutter and closed her brown eyes for a moment, hoping the tears would be unable to fall if she held them behind the gates of her eyelids.

"Lissa."

Pity and sympathy always flavored her sister's words, made them thick as boiled sap. But where syrup was enjoyably sweet, her sister's concern was cloying. Lissa twitched a smile onto her face. She never liked making Annie worry. Her sister spent so much time worrying about her, looking after her. There were only four years between them, but her sister seemed sleek and mature, her words as confident as her carriage. Lissa took a deep breath and coaxed a sentence to the surface. "Hi Annie." Success, with no stumbles, nothing misshapen winging free, and Lissa allowed the deluge of words to emerge, propelled by her previous success. "It's fine. They were teasing me. About the Witch. But its fine. It's fine. I'm fine. F-fine fine f-f-fine." It fell apart there, words repeating, wingbeats against her throat. Up came her hands, gesturing that she was alright, brushing into a soothing motion. Her hands, her body, never let her down. Only her words.

Annie looked unconvinced but held her smile tight on her lips. "I'm sorry they're teasing you."

Lissa frowned, gesturing displeasure, hands slipping into a motion that pushed away her sister's concern. "I. Am. Not. Slow." Lissa spat the words one at a time, making sure they came out clear and untangled, carefully shaping them with lip and tongue and pushing them out, swallowing down the thick danger of something else slipping free. "You. Don't. Have. To…" Her hands flapped in a dismissive motion as frustration choked and smothered her, as her throat filled with flighty twisted words all fighting to escape at once.

Annie's face fell. She pulled her sister into a tight embrace and pressed her face to Lissa's thick, wind-tangled brown hair. "I'm sorry."

And I am not too scared.' Lissa thought, breathing in the scent of spice and flowers that always hung around her sister. *'I'll show them.'*

There were far worse things than a Witch to worry about anyway.

* * *

LISSA WAS CAREFUL AT HOME, keeping the uncooperative flock of her words tightly contained behind pursed lips, bolstered by the lines of concentration that had worn sharp furrows across her forehead. If she imagined her mother to be a sort of sleeping bear that she needed to avoid waking at all times, she could avoid the slap of hands as well as words.

It was her job to get dinner started when she came home, while Annie looked after the laundry from the previous day. Lissa measured three portions of rice into a pan, added water, a bit of salt, and set it to boil. She had started cutting vegetables when she heard the door open, the sharp crack of her mother's shoes against the floor. Lissa bit down on her tongue, resisting the urge to greet her mother. The way her words would flounder could only inspire irritated frustration.

Mother was a tall woman, with hair sculpted into a tight bun that pulled at her face as if trying to stretch out the lines etched there, deep around the corners of her mouth and forehead. She had a face for scowling, that had somewhere along the way forgotten the exact shape of a smile. Mother was the only witch Lissa felt afraid of. She was a being of hard words and sharp expectation. She had to be, Lissa understood that. It was part of her job as she managed the lucrative hotel that attracted foreigners in babbling droves, excited to experience their rugged and beautiful bit of shoreline. But Lissa had always hoped mother would learn to shed that business-skin at the door, take off the manager's mask and become a Mother.

"Mother." Annie emerged from the laundry room to greet

their mother, to give Lissa another moment to quiet the panicked sparrows that made her stomach roil.

Lissa was not scared of their mother, not really. Intimidated, yes. And rightfully so. Lissa had been a 'fretful baby', or so her grandmother used to explain, wrapping warm arms around a red faced and weeping younger Lissa. She had been a fretful baby and grew into an anxious teen. Slow to speak, Lissa had been in the office of every speech therapist her mother could find. Mother was the perfect manager, eloquent and gracious. To have a daughter that struggled so to shape even the most basic sentence wore concern down to frustration, and then emerged irritation. So Lissa learned to speak with her hands. Not proper sign language—that was too much an admission of something being wrong for her mother. It was a collection of gestures Lissa and Annie had pieced together. Their own little language.

Swallowing the desperate starling that had been flapping and flailing in her throat, Lissa set the vegetables to roast and had a smile on her face as she looked up to greet her mother. Her right hand swooped up in a wave as she bobbed her head down, looking away before she had to process her mother's reaction.

Dinners were quiet affairs. Lissa was always afraid to speak in front of her mother, lest an unruly jackdaw of a stutter slip free. She missed her father, his easy smile and booming laugh. When he came home for short stays between fishing runs he would regale them with stories of adventure and improbability. He filled the silences with his warm voice, the shadows with the strength of his presence. Father never pushed her, never looked at her with a shadow of shame or regret in his eyes. Dinners when Father was home were lively, easy. Lissa knew Mother missed Father too in the long times when he was at sea. Mother smiled when Father was around, lost some of the pinched tension around her eyes and mouth.

Lissa waited until Mother set her silverware alongside her plate with familiar precision, the signal that dinner was over and the children should proceed with the cleaning up. Mother would vanish into her office, to make a round of evening calls to the hotel. With Mother safely in her lair, Lissa could exhale, relax the tension that curdled her stomach and curled her spine. Lissa cleared the table, smiling slightly as Annie hummed softly and started washing the dishes. It was a warm moment, a safe stolen bit of time where Lissa could just *be*, listening to her sister's voice and wishing that she too could sing.

The door to Mother's office slammed and both girls flinched. Annie stopped her humming and Lissa slipped out of the kitchen and into her bedroom down the hall. With her door safely shut she did not have to listen to Mother's angry words as she paced, phone in hand. She did not have to make herself small to avoid being noticed. She sat on her bed and hissed one word that slipped free, dark and heavy, a word she did not try to choke back down; "witch."

It was dark and the house was quiet when Lissa slipped on her farm boots, heavy things she wore when she visited her uncle just outside of town to help with his animals, pausing to kick a bit of straw and feather from the last coop cleaning free. It was warm, too warm to go walking in boots along the shore. But it was dark, the sliver that remained of the waning moon hidden behind the gathering of clouds that would result in a morning storm. A moonless, starless night, thick with the foggy promise of rain. It fit her mood, shadowed and stubborn and heavy with a seething anger that was just starting to demand to be noticed. It would also hide the sharp rocks and sharper bits of broken bottle that waited for the unwary, a situation the called for sturdy footwear. Lissa quietly locked the door behind her and walked out into the dark.

The Witch lived to the north, up the rocky shore past all of the summer homes that swayed atop their stilts. Past the sandy beaches. Past the safe places. Lissa knew the shore all the way to the Sweet Sunset, the sprawling vacation home that was always occupied right up until the hurricanes started. But after that she would have to be careful. Unfamiliar rocks and dangerous currents could easily kill her and carry her away, as they had so many foolish and confident people before her. She would be just another story. Another ghost that could be used to attract and scare tourists. Another victim of the Witch.

As far as the seasonal visitors were concerned, Sea Witches were nothing more than a romantic bit of ocean folklore, something that added a bit of flavor to the locale and mysticism to the locals. Nothing real, though. Nothing to be feared. Lissa did not fear the Witch, not really. Respect, perhaps. She had a healthy and practical respect for things that could hurt and kill, fierce wind and crashing waves. Fear was reserved for darker things, things unpredictable and unreliable, like tempers and temperaments. Though she did jump a bit, startled as she reached the end of her narrow street and turned off onto the boardwalk. A flash of eyes caught in the lights of a nearby rental home, wide and unexpected. Lissa frowned, unhappy to find her nerves were not actually made of steel, as the ragged tom cat hissed once before running across the street and into a dark patch of bushes. Lissa bared her teeth and sent a hiss of her own at where the cat had been.

The air was warm, heavy with the threat of rain and so strongly scented with salt and fish and old trash that Lissa could almost taste it. It was unpleasant, and added a bit of speed to her steps as she moved down the boardwalk to the beach. The wood had been replaced last year after a tourist with more enthusiasm than sense had gone through a board that had more flex than its neighbors. Once Lissa felt she was far enough away from the street for casual observation she flicked on her flashlight. It was small, and did not throw much light, but it provided enough that she could avoid stepping on the odd crab and did not stumble on the steps as she reached the end of the walk and made her way down onto sand.

This was the tricky part. Lissa walked across the sand, away from the smooth sandy beach enjoyed by swimmers and sun bathers and started carefully hopping and clambering along a much rockier part of the shore. The ocean was loud, slamming into the rocks as it tried to reach her, tried to shake her free. The wind plucked at her clothes and tried to push her out into the waves. Jaw clenched with concentration and nerves, Lissa slowly made her way along the rocky shore and towards the small inlet she knew should be just ahead. She had never been so bold as to visit the Witch before, but everyone knew where the Witch lived. The Witch was the unsavory neighbor no one wanted in the neighborhood, but no one could do anything about. The Witch was a bit of gossip, a hint of a warning. And, occasionally, a rite of passage. Who would go knock on the Witches door, waiting just a heartbeat before nerves collapsed and they ran away before the door could open?

'I will knock on the door. And I will wait to see who answers.' Lissa grimaced as she slipped a bit, scraping her hand as she reached out to catch herself on rocks rough with limpets and mussels. A quick look confirmed blood was welling out of fierce cuts left by the sharp shells of the shore creatures. She brushed the wound on her pants, angry at the way tears welled from her eyes as blood welled from her hand, as just a bit of both liquids made it to the water below. The world spun a little then, doing its best to buck her off her precarious path. There was a roaring sound that was not the ocean welling up through her ears. She pawed at the wall, desperate not to fall while she regained her sense of stability.

'I will show everyone. I am not slow and stupid. I am not scared.' Her quiet fury pounded like a headache behind her eyes, was echoed in the roar and crash of the surf and the howl of the wind. And then the rocks dropped away, one last step depositing her onto the edge of a sheltered bit of shoreline.

Here the darkness was broken by strange bits of biolumines-cence drifting with the gentle rolling waves closest to the shore. Out deeper it looked like a clear night sky had come down to rest, stars glistening and shooting through the depths. Lissa was mesmerized for a short while, watching the play of light in the water until she heard a door open. That mundane noise in a place that was anything but made her start and shiver and then pointedly pull her spine straight. *'I am not afraid.'*

Perhaps she should have been. The Witch stepped out of the small hut built out of shipwrecks and whale bone that crouched on the shore like a predator, watching. Lissa had expected an old woman, stooped and shambling, the effects of age being the scary part of her story. Never before had any of the stories of the other children mentioned actually seeing the Witch. Chil-dren loved to prove themselves fearless by scaring others with their stories. They could not have avoided telling of the impos-sible and unnatural way the Witch moved, the way the water avoided her feet as if frightened of attracting attention by getting her wet. This was a story that had not been told before and Lissa found her pulse quickening as she stared.

The Witch herself was a long and spindly thing, all hard angles and bone and Lissa could almost hear a skeletons clatter as the Witch stepped out of the house and started to move toward her.

The hollow sound of old bones got louder, leaving the realm of Lissa's imagination for reality as the Witch grew closer, and Lissa could see the strings of small bones and shells that jostled and clattered around her neck. The Witch had a wind-tangled mass of sun-bleached and salt-dried hair. Her skin was leathery with exposure, her eyes narrow from the sun. For all that she was lean, long of limb and tall, the Witch moved with a sinuous and predatory grace across the beach and towards the bit of shore where Lissa stood silent. When the Witch drew close, she bared her teeth in the feral cousin of a welcoming smile, and for a moment Lissa was honestly afraid. The teeth in that grimace looked more suited to the mouth of a shark. Lissa hoped they did not exist in rows, and did not care to look closer, to look inside that mouth, to find out.

There was a churning sensation in Lissa's stomach, a small dark whirlpool of wings and salt and bile and a muscular clench of recognition. There was something in the Witch's narrow, dark eyes that was familiar, that caught her breath as every muscle in her body tightened in preparation. To flee or to fight, Lissa could not tell, but her body went taut and still.

The Witch turned to the side and spat a sound more than a word. A tangle of curses tumbled free, small black birds of storms and shoals and shipwrecks that were carried off into to sea by the wind.

Lissa's mouth went dry and she bit down hard on the sound that tried to escape her own mouth, tried to smother its frantic flapping. Her hands shot up, reflexively shaping a broad 'how'? Her arms were shivery with gooseflesh, the hairs on her arms and the nape of her neck standing at attention. "How?" The word broke free, a giant petrel unfurling in the night and lifting to circle above, her stumbling stutter given vicious, impossible shape. There was a venom to the question, an aggressively assured sense that she had finally found the source of her misery.

The Witches smile curled into something smaller and infinitely crueler. "That is the wrong question. How does the moon pull the waves to follow after her? How does the sun burn and teeth tear? 'How' is not what you want." She spat again, another word that was dark and sharp and burst into a confusion of black wings that flew out and dragged terror and waves behind them.

Lissa could almost taste the bitter flavor of that curse, could almost feel its shape, the brush of its dark feathers. Something rose from the depths of her stomach, burning like bile as it poured up her throat. It carried the glass sharp edge of epiphany and she was terrified to acknowledge it.

But she was done with being scared. She let the thick dark of understanding wash through her, pour out of her throat in long sigh. 'How' wasn't at all what she wanted. *"Who."* The word was stretched long, pulling free of years of stifling of struggling, of trying to squeeze herself into someone else. She hatched there on the shore of the Witch's hut, breaking free of the egg of her shame and sorrow. "Who?" She repeated, an owl's wail.

So this is where Witches were born, hatched under moonlight after being incubated by misery and malice, hardened shell finally cracked by the epiphany of self-reflection and recognition. Lissa panted, mouth hanging open like an overheating, overexcited hound. Her chest felt tight, lungs struggling. She curled tight around herself, but that only made it worse. Lissa stretched out, her back curling back until she was facing the sky with her mouth gaping wide.

The Witch's hand was rough, calloused, with long nails that curled into Lissa's skin as the Witch held her steady. "Shake it off. Scratch it free. It's dead skin, no use to you. Might as well shed it." The Witch's voice was a raven's croak, but lacked any of a raven's friendly inquiry. Lissa's eyes burned with the need to cry, her chest spasmed and heaved. "It's too small for you. Stop trying to make yourself fit."

Lissa screamed, a sound that was raw with anger and seemed to swell and grow, filling the air with dark wings and glittering eyes. It went on and on and when the sound finally staggered to a halt she was left weak and panting, supported only by the Witch's hand.

Her throat felt raw as she tried to swallow, the muscles resisting pulling in after so much pushing out. "What…?"

"Wrong again. You had it right before." There was a rough sneer to the Witch's voice.

"Who." A statement, not a question. Who was she, weak as a hatchling, sweaty and exhausted on the Witch's shore? She could shape it, the whistling edge of the owl's cry. She had been a scared thing, small and hiding in her own skin, stumbling through words and trying to keep the hard wings of her power contained, controlled. It was a power, the way her words were carried on bird's wings, cracked free of the shell of shame that had covered it. Lissa looked at the Witch, a question in her eyes.

The Witch smiled, revealing sharp shark's teeth.

"I'm not afraid of you." Lissa clipped out the words, precise and fierce, Witch to Witch. Her throat swelled with wings and she hissed blackbirds free, lips curled back as she bared her own teeth.

The Witch cocked her head to the side, watching Lissa from one round eye, then another. "No. Now you aren't."

Lissa stepped to the side of the Witch, the edge of the surf lapping at her boots as she made her way around the curve of the little inlet, towards the Witch's house. There was something she had come here to do, before the Witch in her hatched to meet the Sea Witch. There were long dead barnacles decorating the shipwreck wood of the Witch's door. Lissa carefully avoided them as she knocked.

"Scaredy-cat." The boy laughed as he pushed into her, not only refusing to cede her space on the street but actively pushing into her as if she did not matter. "Slow."

"Dummy." Another agreed, genial expression adding to, as opposed to taking from, the cruelty of his words.

Lissa had run into them in the early morning as she came home, as they came out and started ranging through their territory like the feral, infuriating mutts that they were. They swaggered and smiled as they saw her, seeing familiar easy prey, a way to pass the time in the slow and boring morning hours.

Lissa's mouth twisted into a smile, lips pulling back from her teeth. It was not the expression the boys expected, and it made them pause. She allowed the expression to grow, her mouth to open, and spat a curse of vicious shrikes. They unfurled agile wings and dove at the boys who had teased and tormented her for so long.

"W...witch." The first boy looked scared as he stuttered his way through the word, through a new uncomfortable sense of what it meant. Lissa watched someone else struggle with the words battering their throat, her expression detached, almost clinical. She wondered if he felt the brush of bird wings, or just the cruel rake of talons. She wondered if there was just a little bit of Witch in everyone, if only they thought to ask the right question.

The other members of his cruel little pack cowered down, covering their heads as the fast little birds dove and struck them. The first boy stared at Lissa, eyes wide. "Witch." The word was clearer now, clean and simple. If he had caught a taste of the edge of the word he had abandoned it, dropped it before it had a chance to get its claws into him.

Lissa stood still in the street, watching them with hard eyes as the boys broke and ran. Witch. She liked the taste of that word, the silky feel of dark feathers in her throat, the scratch of beak and claw. She carried it with her, the sound and shape and feel of Witch. She sang it sweetly as any wren, reveling in the bright feel of ebullient little passerines as they broke free into the morning light. She brought it home to where Annie was waiting for her, worried.

"Lissa! Where have you been? I was so worried..."

"Annie." Lissa felt a flutter of guilt for sneaking out, for being gone, for growing and changing and not giving Annie any warning whatsoever. Tears, of every description and origin, got tangled up with the birds in her suddenly tight throat. Lissa allowed herself to be pulled close into a hug, to be held, even as wings and claws and beaks battered at her tightly pursed lips. As she remembered the shape of the word 'sister'. It was so gentle, a duckling of a word, soft and warm and clumsy in its affection. She pulled the word around herself like a shawl, like camouflage, and Witch walked inside with her sister.

Witch greeted her mother with a smile that showed a bit of teeth. "Hello, Mother." No birds slipped free with those precise, well-formed words, but her voice was thick with the rustling of wings as they waited. She had walked a night shore to confront a nightmare and hatch under moonlight. There was nothing to scare her here. Not anymore. She was a story they were already whispering, carried by the terrified tongues of the boys.

Who would come knock on *her* door?

NEEDS MUST

They say deep in the forest lives a hag; deep and dark of complexion and demeanor but oh so wise in the ways of this world and of those that brush up against it. They say there is a crook to her back and a lisp to her speech, obviously the result of communing with demons and spirits—unsavory and unhealthy things. They say she is crafty, that you can seek her out for help and end up never leaving. She will always honor her bargains, though they may not always be as palatable as they initially seem.

But I *needed* to see her. My little brother was sick, nothing was helping, and help is what older sisters are for. Mama would not approve, but that is why I had to sneak off before she woke up. I was slipping out the front door even before the cows were stirring and lowing to be milked.

The forest is a different sort of creature in the morning, when the sun is just starting to peek through layers of leaves and poke about on the forest floor. Things stirred as I walked by —crawling things, skittery things. Possibly hungry things. They were never there if I looked directly—they held court in the corner of my eye as I walked along a path that had not seen much traffic. Magical things were not sought out lightly, and the Hag was most assuredly magical. Only the truly desperate traveled there.

And oh, I was desperate. My little brother's breathing labored along with every step I took—there was a familiar wheeze to the way the wind blew through the leaves. He was as pale as the slug I carefully stepped over, the same sort of grey. I did not necessarily need reminders to hurry, but they were everywhere, all around me. I assumed it was the Hag, hounding me with her magic, pulling all the things that made me hurt most to the surface, driving me scared like a stag before his hunters down paths that were covered in the mulch of multiple seasons, scattered with fungus and flower and marked only by the occasional tree bent to point 'go there', a pile of rocks to mark 'come here'.

Until the dark and moist musk of the forest gave way to a clearing, the smell of flowers and still water, and a small house that seemed to have pulled itself together from pieces of the forest around it. I entered through a small break in a circle of stones, walked past a garden filled with flowers organized in neat rows alongside tall spindly greens and bright berries. There were mossy rocks, marking an almost welcoming path up to the door of the house with its sycamore bark sides and crows-nest stick roof.

I have never been the particularly brave one—that would be my older brother. But I was the one that raised my hand and watched in an almost detached horror as it fell against the door in a determined knock. There was a pause, long enough for me to notice my bladder, between when I knocked and when I heard footsteps nearing. And then the door was opening and I was left gawking, there on the doorstep.

She was tall, the woman who answered the door, and lean as a particularly bad winter. But she was far from the physical horror folks made the Hag out to be. Long, dark hair was knotted together in thick strands that hung around her face, adorned with bits of this and that—bone and shell and stone. Her face was darkened by sun and roughened by wind, but its expression was impatient more than cruel. The eyes, though, were what caught me up like a fish and dragged me from my startlement. They were sharp, a clear hazel that seemed to dig into you when you met their gaze.

"Close your mouth before a bee flies in."

I must have looked ridiculous, standing there in clothes my older brother had outgrown years ago, ill fitted to my form but far more useful for trekking the forest path than my own worn gown. My hair had the potential to be filled with all manner of detritus, given the things I had pushed and slipped through on my way here. I could hear humor in her voice, and it brought a flush to my face.

"Pardon, but may I see the Hag?"

Her laugh was a blue jay's shout. "They still call me that, eh? What do you need?"

This was the Hag? She was far too young, far too crisp and clean. She looked like someone I would brush past on the road, not something magical, something Other. My doubt had to have been clear on my face, sure to offend and get me killed, or turned into something unpleasant and amphibious if this was indeed the Hag. But she only sighed and waved me into the house as she stepped aside.

"You might as well take a seat—just push the cat until he moves, there are plenty of other places for a feline to be." The Hag picked up a kettle from the hearth, chasing another, albeit sootier, cat from where it had been lounging before the fire.

I cautiously nudged at the cat on the dining table chair and was grateful when it stretched and hopped down after only a few prods. I perched on the edge of the still-warm chair, uncomfortable—probably more uncomfortable than I would be had I been in the presence of the Hag I had been all but promised. A bit of doubt crept through the back of my thoughts —I did not know if this fairly normal woman could help me. She poured a tea that smelled floral and a bit minty into a slightly chipped pair of cups and set one in front of me.

"Tell me, what do you need? Go ahead and drink the tea— nothing strange there unless you dislike spearmint." She took a sip herself, as if to demonstrate the safety of the beverage, and sat across from me at the cluttered table.

I clasped my hands around the cup, soothing my nerves with its warmth, but not drinking. "It's my brother...he's very sick..."

She lost her amusement at my words, setting her cup down on the table and reaching for a small leather bound book that had been resting to her right and a bit of charcoal. "Describe what is wrong. In detail, girl." My doubt was swept aside by the sudden intensity and light in her eyes. Polite interest had been replaced by something *more*. The skin at the back of my neck prickled.

"He has a cough..."

"Dry? Wet?

"Wet—he coughs things up sometimes..."

"Color?"

"I...I don't know, I have not looked." The Hag grunted and waved for me to continue as she took notes. "He is hot to the touch, complains of being cold. His skin is pale and his heart...his heart does not sound right—it stutters and stumbles."

The Hag wrote for a few long clicks of the clock on the mantle, paused to read over her work and, seeming satisfied, stood and started to gather things from various nooks and crannies of the house. She mixed a bag of herbs, carefully measuring and then sniffing until the result met her approval. She set the bag in front of me, along with a small dark jar. Then she looked down to where I perched uncomfortably on the edge of her chair.

"What is it you want from me?" The words dripped with ritual repetition, hung in the air as if they were expected.

"I want my brother to be well." My voice seemed small in the weighted stillness.

"Are you willing to accept my Terms?"

This...this was the Hag—all sharp eyes and hard lines, her face gone still as she waited for my answer. This was the Hag the stories told about, the bargains that must be struck to secure her service. There was no use in asking what her terms were—the Hag would just repeat her question, so I had been told. I could hear my brother's ragged breathing, his stumbling heart in the silence between us and I answered "yes." A chill danced its way down my spine as...*something* shifted in the air.

The Hag nodded once, accepting. "You will steep these herbs into a tea, and he is to have it three times a day—when the sun first rises, when it is at its highest, and as it sets. This salve is to be rubbed on his chest—warm it first, make it soft. Boil a bit in water when his coughing is at its worst and have him breathe the fumes." She stepped back, motioned towards the door. "Go. Care for your brother. But as soon as his health starts to return, you will return to me."

Arms full, I could not leave that little house fast enough.

* * *

I ALMOST THOUGHT I could forget my deal with the Hag—it was a thing of the forest, of that small house and its strange occupant. I was home, and the Hag's hard eyes seemed so far away, something experienced and explained to Mama, but somehow unimportant now that I was sitting by the fire with a mug of Mama's tea in my hands. My brother's breathing eased, responding to the herbs the Hag had provided. Color returned to his face. And when he sat up and smiled at me one morning I felt something twist and pull in my chest.

My brother was well. I wanted nothing more than to scramble over to his side and pull him into a hug but my feet were already moving, taking me to the front door and outside. It was not me walking; my promise was propelling me towards its completion. It carried me away from my home, down the long woodland path without pause and to the quiet house that belonged to the Hag, who opened the door so I could walk inside.

And suddenly my limbs were my own again, and shaky with the fear being moved like a puppet had inspired.

"What is your name?"

"Sarah." My voice came out far quieter than I wanted.

"Sarah, get some more wood on the fire so I can get supper started. Tomorrow we start working."

TIME WENT strange as soon as you crossed the mossy stones that circled the Hag's clearing. The days seemed longer, the sun taking its time as it ambled across the sky. The nights seemed deeper, darker, filled with unsavory things that lingered to the side, only to vanish if you turned your head.

The Hag caught me looking at the ring of stones somewhere during that first week and smiled. "Useful, that faerie ring. Keeps us in and all the scary out."

I did not want to tell her she was part of the scary. That she seemed a creature of the dark nights and their secrets. But it must have shown, at least a little, on my face.

"The Forest is old, Sarah. I have made my home here for a very long time but It is not always happy with my presence. The stones mark the edges of my land. More than that, they know they are a boundary, and work very hard to maintain it. Now, come here. Identify this row for me."

The Hag had me learning all the plants in her garden—to

make me more useful when she shooed me out the front door after some leaf or petal or root. I was learning her just as much as the various leaves and roots she had me examine. I learned she smelled of citrus soap in the morning, and the herbal blend she kept in a jar by the hearth for smoking by evening. I learned her humor was a bright thing, quick to spark and easy to keep burning if you played with words just right. Her temper revealed itself to be a slow, simmering thing best exposed by my lack of attention. I learned my fear was a thing that made her face grow remote, eyes shuttered as she stepped back to give me space to sort myself out.

I learned her name. It was given to me carefully as the sun was setting and I was stirring something that smelled a little like soup, a little like medicine, over a bed of coals. "Ma'am, what do I..."

"Holly."

I startled, almost slipping off of the little stool with the uneven legs I was perched on. She was sitting there as she had been a heartbeat before, smoking quietly at the table, pale smoke drifting lazily around her. "Pardon?"

"My name is Holly. You might as well use it."

Holly. Sharp and bright. It suited her. "Alright."

"You might want to take the salve off of the fire now. Let it cool."

Her tone was light, amused, and I blushed as I stood and carefully moved the pot from the fire.

* * *

THERE WAS something strangely intimate about knowing Holly's name. It pulled the mystery from her smiles, revealing teeth that collected bits of food like any other. She was still the Hag, a creature of the Forest who could hear the secrets of plants and coax them into assisting with her workings. She could still whistle up a wind and glare a fire into sparking. But she also danced quietly when she thought no one was looking, would sing when she forgot, for a moment, that I was there.

Holly never aged, but I was speeding up to meet her. I grew into my legs—my clothing altered to fit by Holly's nimble fingers. No longer feeling eternally off balance and so easy to startle, I was pleased to note when I started looking like a young woman, with all the curves my mother had promised would appear.

We never crossed out of the stone circle that separated our world from the Forest, from everything beyond. We never needed to. And the nights did not seem as dark as they used to. It was easy to slip into Holly's world and settle like I had been there all along.

* * *

IT WAS a surprise when there came a knock on the door.

Holly looked up from her work mixing tea for the morning and I near stabbed myself with a needle as I startled from the mending. A furrow through the familiar lines of her forehead and a glint in her hazel eyes, Holly stood and opened the door as the visitor started a second attempt.

There was my younger brother, standing there, far older and a little harder around the edges than I remembered, fist raised where it had been interrupted mid-knock.

"Joseph." The shape of his name felt strange, lips and tongue moving in ways they had not for so long, but still remembered.

"Sarah." He started forward, but Holly was there.

The Hag was there, eyes sharp and face hard. "What do you need?"

"I came looking for the Hag. Mama told me she had taken my sister." Had he been searching, my little brother, looking for the sister who had played with pinecones as soldiers, waging war on the acorns, beside him when he was small? The sister that had left him as soon as he got well.

The Hag barked a laugh. "Boy, I did no taking. She bargained her life for yours. Here she stays in return for your good health." It was the way of things, words spoken towards something magical, with intent. I gave my Word, gave myself. And here was the proof of a bargain well made—my young brother grown tall and strong, brave enough to walk the Forest to seek the Hag.

I remembered walking those Forest paths, terrified for Joseph, determined to do whatever it took to make him well. I remembered making my bargain, the feel of it propelling me back to the Hag's door. It felt like a lifetime ago. Before I knew the soft brush of Holly's hair as she leaned down beside me in the garden, the way her hands liked to travel as she thought— petting one cat or the other, fidgeting with her hair. Before the Hag became something irreversibly human.

"Let me bargain to get her back, then."

The Hag went still. It was a stillness that spread through the house, out into the space within the stone circle. It marched gooseflesh up and down my arms. "I cannot break the word of another." Her voice was hard, cold, empty. The sound of it slipped beneath my skin, settled a chill into my bones. Bargains with magical things are not lightly made, not easily broken.

"Sarah?" Joseph beckoned, arms held out to receive me. "Sarah, come home. Mother needs you."

The world can be a cruel thing as it creeps back into time that has been stolen and set aside. It slipped through my veins and pulled at my intent and attention. "Mama?" My mother, with her soft smile and gentle eyes. The strength in her arms, in her voice. Rocking me to sleep when I was very small, plaiting my hair, helping me wash the vegetable garden from my feet. I had never said goodbye.

It was an old thing, the drive to help one's parent, old as the earthy magics the Hag coaxed and nurtured. It sent my heart thundering, dried all the moisture from my mouth. Mother needed me. There must have been something in my expression as I turned to look at the Hag. At Holly. I could feel the way conflict pulled at muscles, clenched my jaw, dug furrows across my forehead. The Hag did not blink her hard eyes, did not offer me anything related to a way out of this.

I reached out, took my brother's hand, and broke my word. I could feel it snap, pulling at my muscles like a cramp. But no magic kept me from crossing the circle of stones. No voice called out to order me back. No one called out to *ask* me to come back. The Forest was a quiet place, seeming to watch as I walked a path I had not seen for many years. I was taller now, needing to duck branches that had seemed so high up before, stepped over rocks that had felt like mountains. I could name the mosses and brambles and tiny flowers scattered about and with that realization the Forest became far less frightening that it had been.

My house was smaller than I remembered, paler. The front door was badly in need of painting. My mother was smaller than I remembered. Paler. Hunched over herself in the old chair she has always occupied by the fire. But she was not spinning or knitting this time. Her clever hands seemed twisted as the reaching twigs of the forest and they were tangled in the blanket spread over her lap.

All of the ways the Hag had trained me let me recognize that my mother was slipping away. It was apparent in the colors of her skin, the way it sat on her bones. It was visible in the way she shook as she reached to pull the blanket closer to her. It drifted through the raspy roughness of her voice as she greeted my brother. She greeted me with a surprised smile and I reflexively took note of worn, discolored teeth. This was nothing I could fix. There was nothing in the Hag's deep bag of tricks that could make my mother well again. She was not sick—she was merely old.

"Hello, Mama." I folded my legs and sat at her feet, as I had years ago, rested my head on her bony knee. Tried not to notice the way the scent of her reminded me of the way leaf mulch smelled in the fall, of death and decay.

"Sarah. My Sarah." She rested a hand on my head and I closed my eyes.

* * *

I GATHERED plants to make into teas to help my mother sleep, to soothe pain that was determined to linger. I sat with her in the evening and told her stories in front of the fire, let her card her stiff fingers through my hair. I slept poorly, my mind grasping after ethereal things spun of dream stuff, leaving me disoriented and filled with disquiet in the morning. I was a stranger in my old home, my younger brother casting glances at me as I was prepared herbal teas for my mother, when he thought I would not notice. My older brother, I was told, had moved to the next village over, started a modest farm with his wife. A wife! The things I had missed. The family I felt so disconnected from.

I missed the yowls and purrs of the cats, the calls of creatures that wandered the Forest. I missed the sound of Holly's voice as she sang quietly, as she scolded a feline for plopping down and rolling in her most recent batch of herbs. I loved my mother, my brothers, but I was watching someone else's life, off to the side, present but not involved. I was a ghost in a home that had not been mine for quite some time.

"Sarah!" The sound of my name startled me from my thoughts. I looked up, and dropped the herbs I had been carefully gathering to the ground in front of me. I was very different than I had been when I slipped away in the night, holding my older brother's cast offs tight against my skinny frame. But Benjamin, he had not changed. There were lines on his face I did not remember, the shadow of stubble along his familiar chin, but his smile was familiar as he walked towards the house, as was the merry light to his eyes. I hardly realized I had moved until I was pressed against his chest, arms around him, breathing in the hay, horse, and sweat smell of him as I was embraced in return. "I did not expect to see you here, Sarah."

I pulled away and out of his arms. "Mama needs me."

"Joseph needed you. Mama needs you." Benjamin reached out and mussed my hair a bit, affectionately, before carefully smoothing it back into place. I resisted the urge to follow after that comforting touch like a cat. "When will you pay attention to what you need, little sister?"

Helping Joseph. Helping Holly. Helping Mama. Those were easy roles to fill, expectations I could examine and act accordingly to fulfill. But what did I need?

I looked at Benjamin. "Could you help me bring these herbs in? There is some soup on the fire—it is not thickened but I could spoon a bowl for you if you are hungry."

Benjamin sighed but chose not to point out my deflection.

WHAT DID I NEED? The question swirled through my head, a clumsy cat chasing its tail. Thickening soup, baking bread, serving dinner to my brothers, my mother—it was comfortable work, comforting. The way my brothers teased each other, the way Mama and I both protested the moment a bit of food was launched in addition to Benjamin's verbal sally—it was warm, a sense of family I could wrap around myself like a blanket.

Settled before the fire after dinner, the sweet rosehip and honey tea Holly had favored lingering on my tongue, I could hear a bit of coyote song in the distance. Their yips and shouts and shivery screams had been so much louder settled by the fire in the house in the Forest. The first time I heard them, so near to the edge of the circle of stones, gooseflesh had marched up and down my arms and Holly had laughed, the sound mingling with the wild things, the night things. The memory made me smile, my toes curl in contentment. I had touched too much of the wild spaces, and they had touched me back, adding to me. My warm blanket of family seemed small, a child's beloved accessory. No less beloved, even though it was no longer enough to cover myself in.

Benjamin dropped a hand onto my head as he wandered over to wish me a good night, as he reached to take Mama's hand and help her to bed.

Coyote song mixed with the quiet snores of Joseph where he had fallen asleep in his own chair beside the fire. I dropped a kiss to Joseph's forehead, smiled as he shifted and snorted in his sleep, and slipped out the door.

I needed a trail through the Forest that was lit by moonlight and softly phosphorescent fungus. I needed the calls of owls, the singing of coyotes and the rustling of things unseen off to the side. I needed a mossy ring of stones keeping guard over a house that looked thrown together from the Forest around it.

I needed the smell of dirt, the smell of herbs being dried, simmered, smoked. I needed the complaints of cats and a bit of song while I worked. I needed a garden loud with bees and rich with lessons. My feet carried me to the Hag's door and I knocked with far more assurance than I had years ago.

The Hag opened after the first knock, as I lifted my hand for the second. Hard eyes regarded me from their place in a dirt-scuffed and familiar face. A shy smile curled my lips as I shoved my hands into the pockets of my brother's old pants.

"Good evening, I am looking for Holly."

The hard lines of the Hag's expression loosened, something I assumed was only noticeable to those who had spent time studying every shape that dramatic face attempted. "What do you need?"

"I need to learn; I need to grow." All of my thoughts,

condensed down into such small, small words, putting a name to the nagging itch I had carried around my head since following Joseph home. They might know me as another Hag in the forest, to seek out when help was needed. Sarah might fade until no one remembered her but my brothers, but that was alright. I would learn herbs and quiet magics here where the stones stood guard and the Forest glared in at night only to be chased off with laughter.

Holly offered me her hand, silently, and I took it.

TRANSPOSITION

I keep dreaming that I am drowning. The light filters down through murky water, through the long waving fingers of kelp. My startled shout dances free as a giddy chain of bubbles making their way to the surface as I fall deeper to where it is darker. I gasp at the water, struggling to breathe, limbs flailing and doing nothing more than tangling me in the forest of kelp, confusing up from down as I thrash until I no longer know which way is the surface. I cease struggling, close my eyes, and inhale the ocean…

…and I wake. Every time. I can still taste salt water in my mouth, can still feel its sting in my sleep-grimy eyes. The light of early dawn creeps in through my window with some of the same murky weakness that filtered down from the surface to the ocean depths. It takes me a few minutes to move with enough coordination to turn off my alarm. Moving freely in the open air of my bedroom in the early morning is a sharp contrast to the thick struggles of my underwater dreams. Slow to wake, to make it back to reality. Every time.

An absently thorough once over with my toothbrush while I wait for the shower to warm up clears away a lingering bit of brine that kept trying to confuse my senses. A blast of mouth wash dispelled the lingering ghost grit of churned up sand. The shower itself was the last piece to the ritual that pulled me back to reality, water hot and steamy and smelling of absolutely nothing washing over me, washing away salt and cold. Far more aware of my surroundings, and the fact that I remembered I had a schedule, I rushed through shampooing and rinsing my short dark hair. Soaping as thoroughly as I could manage without losing my balance amidst the exertion I then sped through a rinse, turned off the water and grabbed a towel. One day I would give myself a little more time between alarm and leaving. One day. I had been telling myself that for most of my high school years. Unfortunately restful sleep was in short order, lost somewhere between homework and sports and deep vivid dreaming once I did manage to lay my head down. I ran a hand through my wet hair, threw on some clothes, and thanked whoever might be listening that was the extent of teenage male grooming expectations.

The smell of coffee lured me downstairs, dressed in un-torn jeans and a plain t-shirt for my weekend shift at the bookstore. My hair was a mess of damp tufts and enthusiastic little spikes from where I had run my hand through it and pulled a shirt over it. My mother passed me a comb with my coffee cup, unspoken encouragement to put a bit more attention towards putting myself together for work. I ducked my head sheepishly and mumbled thanks before taking my first magnificent sip of coffee of the day.

"You're welcome." My mother's voice was soft, deep, her vowels curled around the edges with an accent as familiar to me as it was exotic to my friends. Her large, dark eyes and the sharp angles of her face did nothing to dispel the image of some fairy princess slumming it with us mortals. Mom was mom. My friends like to try and get me to tell stories of how my parents met, how she had managed to end up with a rough around the edges businessman like my dad. When I was young, I adored the attention, the idea that there was something special about me, about my family. As I grew, and started to notice the looks my friends sent my mother's way when they thought my attention was elsewhere, it just became embarrassing.

"What shift are you working today?"

Mornings were not my forte, and conversation sometimes difficult to navigate before caffeine effectively cleared out mental cobwebs. I pulled my mind back from the wandering it was prone to, taking a sip of coffee to hopefully hide how I had to chase down the answer to her question. What she was really asking was would I be home when Dad got back from his trip, if she would have an ally amidst the swell and burst of his temper if things had not gone as he had wanted. I hated having to let her down. "I have a long shift today, working straight through until five." I would not be home when Dad got home. I would not be here to deflect and soothe and smooth things over. Hopefully things went well, hopefully it was a productive conference, a business trip worth taking. Dad feeling like he had wasted money was a fearsome beast.

I watched Mom's hope crest and then break into resignation, her dark eyes going unreadable. It hadn't always been like this. I remembered more in the way of smiles when I was younger, Dad's booming voice rumbling into a laugh, Mom curled against his side. Cheese aged well, as did wine. My parents' marriage had not.

And sometimes I was afraid it was my fault, that I was the ingredient that threw off the recipe to their happy marriage.

"Do you have plans after?"

Will you stop by to check on things, is what she was actually asking, the question caught in the purse of her lips, traced in the lines on her face. "No, I was coming home. I thought I could cook us some dinner?" Hopefully tacos would please everyone.

"That would be perfect."

There was a bit of silent puttering, me finishing my coffee and practically inhaling a banana. Mom finished the dishes from her own early breakfast and put away dishes left to dry last night. As I set my cup in the sink, Mom presented her cheek for a kiss.

"See you a little after five" I promised, planting an unnecessarily silly kiss on her cheek and backing away before her affectionate swat could land.

There were few benefits to living in a coastal tourist trap over the summer, but having employment within easy walking distance was one of them. The bookstore could only keep me summers when their business surged along with the temperature, but that worked perfectly with my attempt at a work/school balance. It was a small store, local interest titles as opposed to best sellers decorating the window, a single wooden door with its cheerful handwritten 'Open' sign inviting me in.

It was early yet, but the air-conditioning was humming and hissing from its perch in the window at the back of the store. Even a hardened local like myself appreciated the cool, and for visitors and tourists it was the carrot that lured them in to visit and the balm that encouraged them to stay for a while. I waved to Tara, the owner of Treasured Pages, who was at her place settled behind the counter, and slipped through the Young Adult section and through the door into the back room. My employee lanyard was one of three tangled on the hook by the desk where we all sat for our breaks. Lanyard over my head and initials on the time clock, I was officially on the clock. And officially about to spend a couple hours shelving yesterday's shipment.

I dream of drowning, even when daydreaming. The regular rhythm of moving book from cart to shelf was soothing, familiar, and my brain often takes to wandering while my hands are occupied. The hum of the air conditioning created a cocoon of white noise, buffering me from the rest of the world. The cool air from the unit pulled with it a cold current of water slipping through the depths, tugging at me, taking me along with it. Down to where the kelp rock and dance in the waves, twisting and chasing each shift in the current. I rock with them, lulled as complacent as a babe in a cradle. Drowning was easy here, drifting and sinking held by the water...

The door opened with a crack, snapped back on hinges worn loose and never replaced. I came back to the bookstore with a choke that I could pass off as a cough, my lungs working to realize they were breathing air and not water.

"Hello! How are you today?" Tara's friendly voice greeted.

I shoved the last book on my cart into its place on the shelf and made my way up to the front of the store, to see if Tara needed me to help with this customer. The old clock on the wall behind the counter shocked me into stopping and blinking. How had I lost more than an hour back in the shelves, in the waves? My brain scrambled to catch up with the day as I plastered the retail smile I had perfect onto my face and continued walking.

"Is there anything I could help you with?"

A tourist, smelling of sunscreen and bug spray, poked around at the collection of books on shipwrecks and hauntings that we had on display. "Just looking."

Just looking, just pausing in the cooler air, just looking for WiFi.

"Let me know if there is anything I can help you find!" Tara smiled her thanks and nodded me back to my busy work. She could manage the front for a bit longer.

A lot longer. It became apparent that today was going to be one of those slow days that retail folks both love and dread. Tara sent me home early with an apologetic and familiar chat about needing to save hours when we were this slow. I hung my badge back on the hook, scrawled my initials under the time on the staff calendar, and started the short walk home.

It was a surprise to see Dad's silver SUV in the driveway out front — he rarely came home from a business trip early. But it wasn't until I heard his voice from the end of the driveway, caught the edge to his still-indistinct words, that I began to hurry. Yelling was new. Dad's temper usually burned cold and sharp. This was hot and harsh.

I interrupted something as I let myself in, the hairs on my arms startled into attention. Dad stood, feet braced and slightly apart, hands clenched at his sides. The tension in the hall between the front door and the rest of the house was thick and sour, pressing tight against us as we stood still, assessing each other.

"We will talk later." Dad broke the silence first, pushing his way through the discomfort with a grim determination, lips curling at the end of his words.

If Dad was the bull in this emotional china shop, Mom was an elegant counter. Her eyes had gone hard, her body so still, but she nodded ever so slightly at his words. Her acknowledgement was kept from being a concession of defeat by the serenity of her expression. So aloof, so untouchable — mom seemed carved out some something far sturdier than flesh. Not unyielding, that was all in the hard lines and stiff spine of Dad. "We will. I believe we have words yet between us, you and I."

"Sorry to interrupt." The ocean roared in my ears and my face burned with a mix of anxiety and embarrassment. The smell of seaweed rotting in the hot summer sun filled my nostrils, blocking the faint floral scent of the air fresheners Dad preferred that usually tinged the house. It was hard, having both of their attention on me when the emotional tangle just made me want to scurry up to my room, close the door, and wait for the storm to pass.

"How was work?" Dad was attempting to coax the normal flow of things back into the house with his words, but his body language still resembled that of a feral tom cat intent on chasing an intruder from his territory.

But I was willing to play along. Anything to try and quell the tension that had enveloped the house like a violent tide. "Not bad. Slow, so I was cut. But that's ok, really. More time at home and I can actually cook a proper dinner."

"Tacos?" Mom allowed a small smile to creep onto her face.

"Tacos." I answered with my own tentative smile. "Everyone likes tacos, right?"

Dad snorted, finally diffusing the last bits of the previous tension and discomfort. I moved forward to claim my hugs usual post-work greeting hugs from both parents, needing that bit of a child's comfort and reassurance. It wasn't a perfect family, but it was all I had and all I knew and I feared it was becoming as impermanent as the morning fog.

Tacos were serious business if I was cooking, involving far more fish than non-coastal folks would consider proper, and a lot more chipotle than was honestly necessary. But I loved the rhythm of cooking, the spices, putting it all together in a plated presentation that would be the envy of fine Mexican dining. I could hear my parents taking out in the dining room, but no voices raised too high and hard in anger, so I let the art of the kitchen soothe me. After adding thin slices of marinated radish to each plate of tacos, I collected a plate for each parent and made my way into the dining room, proud as any child with an art project to share.

I entered the dining room just in time to see Dad pull back his hand, to see the red start to bloom across Mom's cheek. Dad blinked once, looking at his hand as if wondering where it had gotten the order to strike. There was a chaotic mix of horror and anger in his eyes, and then he noticed me standing there, mouth and eyes open wide.

Mom straightened, seemed taller. "Remember your word,

Aaron." Her words cut through the still shock of the scene and the room seemed to hold its breath.

Reflexively I placed the plates onto the table, a desperate bid for normalcy as my brain tried to catch up with what my eyes were seeing. I had known things were getting bad. But I did not think we had gone beyond harsh tones and words and directly into hitting. I could feel stability and normalcy being sucked away in wild outgoing tide. Appetite turned instantly to nausea as my stomach churned and I stared at my parents.

Instead of acknowledging Mom's words or his actions, Dad turned his back on us and went upstairs. It was not until the door to his office slammed shut that Mom turned to me, her dark eyes flat and cold. I did not know her then. There was nothing warm in her eyes, her expression, nothing of the mother that sat up and joked with me over tea at night or who walked the beaches with me on lazy mornings. I flinched away from her before I managed to scramble after my self-control. Mom looked inhuman, terrifying, but she was still my mother. She was still Mom.

"We need to talk, Ross. Come with me." Her voice sent chills dancing down my spine. It lacked any emotion, her accent rolled through the words without gracing them with the life and personality is usually brought.

I was torn, wanting to check in on Dad, worried about whatever it was that had worn him so thin he had snapped. But Dad's office was not a space where I was wanted or welcome, and I did not think that would have changed as a result of what had just happened. So I followed Mom, out past the large deck with its Adirondack-style chairs and rarely-used grill. We made our way down the boardwalk, over the dunes and to the beach. Mom was barefoot, not having bothered to put on shoes. I worried the midday sand would be too hot on the soles of her feet, but she did not seem to notice when the boardwalk ended and the beach began. This was not one of our comfortable, companionable walks. I was walking in her wake, powerless to turn away, too frightened to disobey. As inexorable and uncaring as the tide, Mom walked for what felt like hours, stopping only when we came to a battered old abandoned pier.

"I met your father here." She stood beside one of the old pilings, looking out to sea while one hand brushed along the colony of barnacles that had established itself some time ago. "I was hurt, caught up in old lines and half-rotted nets. Young and panicking and just this side of drowning. He saved me. He pulled me from the sea and untangled my flippers."

"Wait…what?" Flippers? Nothing had made sense since I had walked in to see my Dad hitting my Mom. But this…this was beyond surreal. I must have heard her wrong. The ocean sent wave after wave our way, churning past the pilings to just touch our toes before slipping back. There was a rhythm to it, one I had always found soothing, even with my dreams of drowning. The ocean was a constant, reliable both in its beauty and ferocity. I wanted to be lulled by the crash and slide of the waves, I wanted to allow the ocean to hold me close and whisper quiet comfort in my ear, to drown out the strangeness of my mother's words, her tone. Flippers. "What do you mean, flippers?"

"Surely you have books on selkies in that bookstore of yours." Mom's tone was dismissive, ignoring my flustered confusion.

"Yes. Fairy tales. Stories. Things told to tourists to get them to fall in love with the romantic and the legendary. To get them to spend money" I was babbling, drowning in words as surely as I drowned in water in my dreams. There were selkie stories. We were an island, a tourist destination. The sea was romantic, mysterious. And what was more romantic than stories about selkies saved and taken for wife, who learned to love their human husbands? What was more mysterious than stories of seal skins hidden away for generations, found accidentally allowing a seal maiden to return to the sea? This mundane little tourist trap of an island that was the center of my world could not possibly be peopled by selkie, by seals who sometimes wandered about as people. The idea made no sense. There was no way my mother was a creature of myth. "There are no selkies in real life. There just…aren't."

Mom ignored my babbling, apart from raising an almost amused eyebrow. She continued with her story, a story that was determined to be heard now that she had started, now that she had cracked open the box it had been locked inside of for so long. "I offered him myself as wife in thanks for saving me, as was proper." Mom looked at me now, a sly smile curved along her lips. "Fey things are known for making deals, and humans are wise to take heed to the words they use, the terms they set." The rhythm of her speech matched the roll that had always been to her accent, finally making her sound foreign, not just strange. Alien, not exotic. "I would be his wife, love him and look after him, as long as he always took care to treat me kindly. As long as he never turned to me in violence. He broke his word today, Ross."

I wasn't drowning, I had drowned. I was choking and terrified beneath the crush of her words, the dark glint of her eyes, the shift in her posture that made her seem so much larger than she had been before. So much *more*. My chest heaved but my lungs drew in no air. My limbs wanted to drag and flail, to push away the pressing weight that had crashed down with my mother's words, to push away the rushing sensation that seemed to have started at my toes and rushed towards my brain, urging me to close my eyes and let the current take me where it willed. And beneath it all was a smug sense of having *known*. She had been telling me all along with her soft songs and barefoot walks along the shore, if only I had known to listen to that corner of my brain that always told me Mom was something different, someone special. I tried to focus on the crash of the waves, the familiar rhythm, as if it would somehow smother the strange story my mother was weaving.

"You were my treasure, my pup, my boy. I was so excited when I was carrying you. I sang you the songs of my people, our people. I had a midwife with me to deliver you at home, away from the poking and prying hospitals. One of my sisters, come ashore to welcome you." Her sly smile returned. "Birthing is woman's business, and your father was happy to keep it so. So when a little pup came into this world, eyes wide and startled, I was able to coax you out of your skin, to secret it away, and present your father with a perfect baby boy."

She bared her teeth, which had gone sharp and feral, a leopard seal's mouth in my mother's face. Nausea choked me and I had to work not to stumble back a step. "Your father destroyed my skin. He wanted to make sure I could never leave. He did not raise a hand to me then, oh no, he kept his word and sold it to be made into clothes. Cut and torn and stitched to cover and protect someone else, dead to me. The magic gone, my magic gone. But your skin, my baby, my pup, yours has been safe and secret." Hands that curled like claws, which had sprouted the nails to match, pulled at the aging piling, dislodging barnacles and bits of wood until she removed a folded bit of fur. Her body seemed to ripple, a wave going through and disrupting her solidity and stability.

I wanted to pay attention to Mom, the changes I wanted to find some way to explain away. But I could not help but fixate on the scrap of fur in Mom's hands. My heart galloped in my chest, gooseflesh crawled up and down my arms, my back. My mouth went dry and I could smell nothing but the murky salt of the sea. I was reaching out before I consciously acknowledged the action, desperately wanting. Craving. Needing.

Mom was smiling as she handed over the fur. My fur. It was a feral smile, all teeth and anticipation.

It was like seeing clearly, thinking clearly, for the first time in my life taking that damp bit of fur into my hands. The absentminded fog that had danced along the edges of my thoughts and dreams for as long as I could remember dissolved as everything snapped into focus. It's like I had been split between two places, my daily teen life and the piling where my skin shifted and slipped with the tides. I had not been drowning, I had not been dreaming, I had been one person in two places. The quiet song of my skin had been calling to be all this time, I had just not known how to listen, how to answer.

I spread it out, marveling how it shimmered softly in the late afternoon sun, how it stretched and grew, accommodating how I had grown since we had last been together. I looked up at Mom, feeling her at the edge of my consciousness in a way that was new and fascinating. She felt muted somehow, diminished, and I realized it was because she was without her skin. Dad had destroyed some essential part of her when he allowed her skin to be destroyed. I wanted to wrap her in my own skin, to let her, a wild thing too long caged, flee out into the sea.

She saw my look and shook her head, teeth clenched in a grimace of denial. She was softer again, smaller, human. My skin had sang to her as she stood there, like calling to like as it told me her story. Our story. But the skin was mine, back in my hands, and she would not take it from me. I was defensive with a ferocity that terrified me, unwilling to be parted from the treasure in my hands. Willing to fight back if anyone tried to take it from me. Willing to fight off my own mother if need be. There was a feral edge to this new-found magic, this corner of my being, that was frightening in its primal simplicity. There was a whole catalog of emotion and sensation I was still trying to sort through, and again I found myself drowning.

"Momma..." The diminutive slipped free on a voice gone unsure. I was a little thing again suddenly, unsure, and the world was much larger than it had been an hour ago. I wanted nothing more than to be folded into my mother's arms, sang to, told everything would be fine. It was a hard thing, being a child wanting his mother but also something strange and new that wanted nothing more than to crash into the waves and *go*. My breathing was shallow and hitched, indecision pulling tears from my eyes.

"My pup." Mom opened her arms and I took the handful of steps that put me into them. She sang to me, quietly, little wordless songs like the ones that had always calmed me when I was young, when I woke from dreams of drowning.

Except they weren't dreams of drowning at all. They were the hopeful, lonely song of my skin calling to me. Looking for me. Wishing for the sea. I was torn between answering that call of my skin and diving down deep into the sea and staying curled in my mother's arms.

"Go on, little one. Find treasure in the deeps, hunt and chase and explore. Learn the song of the moon on a clear night, the roar of a storm, the chortle of a game of chase. Find your sisters and brothers out in the waves, on distant shores. Learn how to coax a maid to you. Learn how to sink ships. Learn what freedom tastes like." Her arms tightened around me, her voice hardening. "Never give that freedom away, not without a fight. Obligation is a heavy collar to bear. Find another way to honor and repay a favor. Never give up your skin."

I could not imagine giving it up, now that I had it. It was joy given tangible form in my hands, that feeling of stretching for the first time after deep restful sleep. I was finally awake, and I was itching to move. It was a strange sort of adulthood and independence that came with my skin. The need to be out in the ocean exploring and experiencing was an overwhelming urge that crashed over me like the waves of a fast returning tide with each heartbeat. Selkies were never made to be out of the ocean, not for as long as I had. Mom's words, her intensely encouraging tone, had soothed the worst of the conflict between human rearing and newfound selkie magic. Her expression was fierce and proud, its smile toothy and determined. In a strange way, Dad had set her free this evening. Mom could go where she wished now, my Dad having broken the word that bound her to him. I would see her again. The sea was in her blood as much as it was in mine. We would find each other on rocky shores and I would tell her tales and we would laugh and maybe we would even venture ashore in search of the perfect taco.

I kissed my mother on the cheek, the faint song of her selkie blood, muted without its skin, whispering to me one more time. And then I was folding my skin around me like a blanket, feeling a storm surge rush to my veins, and then I was running into the surf, flippers pushing me along the packed sand of the shore until it dropped off and I was swimming.

Light filtered down through the water, dimming as I dove, testing muscles I had only dreamed about before as I sought out rafts of waving kelp. I did not struggle to swim, to breathe — my body had been made for this, had been dreaming of this for so long. The ocean was in my blood, had been calling to me for my entire life. And now I could finally answer.

GRIEVE AND RELEASE

Magic is knowing. It is watching and listening and sometimes asking. Cajoling the bits and pieces of the world to work together. Magic is a puzzle spread out on the table, but there is always that one piece that has been lost by the cat. Witches are whisperers, are artists. They are always looking for that lost piece, and they know better than to discipline the cat.

My mother taught me the secrets of plants and stones and how to read the wind and the temperaments of the weather. The greenhouse she used to tend with joy was my favorite classroom. From calendula to mugwort to arugula to pole beans— my mother taught me the way of growing things. How to listen to them and to use them. I could make an arnica salve by the time I was eight, singing to the herbs as I unfused the oils just like mom did. Ours was a down to earth magic. She taught me to always have salt and pepper packets with me, just in case I needed a quick protective circle.

This had always been a house of witches, for generations now. Mom had learned in the same greenhouse from her mother. And *her* mother had been the one to build the greenhouse to begin with. The house had grown with the family, but it had always been ours. It knew us. It was quieter now, with just me, the semi-feral cat named Waffle that wandered the garden, and the bones of the tiny kitten Nugget that rested under the threshold. Nugget was not one for conversation, but I always left him cream on full moons and holidays, just as my mother had taught me.

My mother also taught me the words, the rhythms, and the herbs for calling a familiar. I had taken notes, added scribbled thoughts in the margins. Academically, I knew what needed to be done, and had been trying to get what worked on paper to work in practice. This morning had been another failure. Magic is learning which words slip into which sentence, match with intent and herb. I had the cookbook; I was trying to sort out the right recipe for what I wanted. What I needed. I stared hard at the sage that had burned down to a stub. There had been no omen in the smoke, no hint in the scattering of bones spread across the kitchen table. Day 30. Still no familiar. I could almost hear my mother laughing. Standing, spitefully leaving my failed puff of magic to disperse as it damn well wanted by not putting my tools away, I grabbed a bucket and walked out the door.

I was frustrated and wanted to be outside. How could I fail so persistently at such a common spell? Such a simple one. I could find lost things. The spells for abundance that I wrote on the seeds of my melons always ripened perfectly. My cooking was a whirlwind of spices aimed at intent, and those intents carried through. I had worked with the full moon, with the dark. I tried morning, noon, and midnight. I have used every liminal space I could think of—edge of sea to edge of woods and even one time on the very *very* edge of a very high hill. And still my workings towards a familiar fizzed with depressing regularity. It refused to provide me a result for my work. I was at a loss.

The neighbor down the street had a patch of blueberries. They were tended with love and as a result tasted like the best parts of summer. I used to pick strawberries with my mom every time they burst into season, used to stir them into the best sort of jam to savor and store for the cold, dark months. The blueberries my neighbor grew attracted me in a similar way. They were a season distilled and allowed that season to bubble up with every taste when it was needed most. There was an alchemy to jamming. Fruit, sugar, heat, and fond memories.

Making blueberry jam reminded me of my mom, but at least the fruit was wrong to hit the memories hardest. I refused to gather strawberries for jam anymore. Going alone was too sharp.

My neighbor and I have known each other for some time. We both grew up here in our rambling houses out in the middle of nowhere rural New York. His family moved in when I was about five, but his parents didn't mind their son out chasing frogs with the neighbor girl. There were some comfortable rural liberties we took with each other. I could walk up his driveway, nod at the house in greeting, and go around back to where the blueberries grew, and I did so regularly throughout the blueberry season.

It was warm today, and sunny, but the neighbors old white cat joined me as usual, ambling alongside as I worked, sometimes chasing a grasshopper or the rare frog. I fell into the rhythm of harvesting, the actions so familiar my brain took to wandering, thinking about other berries and different sunny day. The nip to my calf from the old white cat was unexpected, startling me out of thoughts of fingers sticky with strawberry juice.

'You are thinking too much on *then*' said a sharp flick of just the very tip of her tail. 'Pay attention to now' she recommended with a quick flattening of her ears.

"Oh, hush." I appreciated and respected the old queen, but I showed it in my own way. A sort of verbal clawless swat to show I was paying attention to my elders, but that I didn't have to be happy about it. The straightforward company of the cat was comforting after the frustration of the morning. Cats tell you like it is, no elaborate linguistic gymnastics. The language of cats is carefully sparse and elegant and suited my temperament just fine. I would have liked a cat as a familiar, but I was not rude enough to ask the old queen. She was quite obviously fond of my neighbor.

A ghost of strawberry sugar still lingered on my tongue. I slid a perfectly ripe blueberry into my mouth, bit down and let the tart flavor drown out remembered sweetness. I planned to can them to enjoy when the snow is heavy on the ground, to cook them down to a syrup to pour decadently over pancakes. It was a hot and humid day, but I always enjoyed a bit of hearth work, and anything was better than sitting back down to try, again, to try and sort out what I was doing wrong.

"Alright. I am going to head back."

The old queen flicked the very tip of her tail dismissively as she settled into a bed of tender, young grass at the base of a blueberry bush. She closed her eyes, but there was a quiet and companionable purr to send me on my way. 'Remember what I said, kitten' was carried on the weight of her sigh as she settled into her rest, the way she stretched her toes once, slowly. She had dispensed her wisdom. Whether or not I paid attention to it was on me.

My neighbor was waiting for me, sitting on his front steps with his younger cat, a leggy orange little thing that was busy exploring the tomato plants growing in containers all around them. "Hello."

"Hi." I lifted my full blueberry bucket in greeting.

"Beautiful day, isn't it?" He pushed some of his long hair out of his face as he spoke.

If I was a witch, this fellow was a fox. All lean angles and sharp smiles. And he possessed an infinite sort of quiet patience that did a magnificent job of masking a beautifully biting wit.

That wit was often hobbled by the shy awkwardness of someone who doesn't get out around other people much. Witch to hermit solidarity—neither of us had any idea of what to do with something like small talk and we let the long silences fill with birdsong and cicada screams without stress. We were forgiving with each other, even if we did very often fall back on safe conversational gambits like the weather.

"I could do with less sun, but yes" I agreed. "Good berry picking weather."

We both nodded appreciation of the weather and spent a handful of silent moments smiling slightly as we watched his kitten try to reach the cabbage white butterfly that was making its way through the tomatoes.

He broke the silence, tilting his head to the side and asking, "have you been over to the swamp yet?"

"I mean, it is a short walk" I gestured past his house towards where the frogs were singing and shouting with a loose sort of wave.

"No, not our swamp. There is one just a couple miles away. Trillium Swamp. It's a public trail, but no one knows it is there, really, so it is never busy. I think you might like it."

The flow of words caught me just a little off guard. Something must have shown in my face because he smiled shyly and his kitten dropped her mouth open in a huffing laugh that was definitely directed at me.

"Thank you. I will have to give it a shot." I had been scrambling to sort out a direction, something to try, and it seemed the universe had given up on being subtle and was taking the direct route. It's not that we rarely spoke, it's just our conversations were usually comfortably superficial. Our silences were generally much more nuanced and richer.

The current silence ambled on as I spent a minute or three chasing after words and trying to figure out what to do with eye contact before finally admitting I had exhausted my conversational supply for the day. I raised my bucket of berries again in a sort of friendly salute, smiled, and made my way back down the road to my long and rambling driveway.

I would give Trillium Swamp a shot. My tea had not predicted anything remarkable today, and the bones had been irritatingly unhelpful. But I had been impatient enough with the brewing and drinking of my morning cup that my mother would have been embarrassed with my clumsy disregard of portents. I had been less than focused as I tossed the bones across the kitchen table. I had forgotten to move my mug, and a vertebra had bounced. Mom would have been horrified, probably would have said something about how she had trained me better. I ground my teeth a bit as I swallowed roughly. Portents aside, I had been having terrible luck calling a familiar and a change in scenery might be nice. A little distraction.

I kicked off my shoes once inside, nudging them so that they rested in their place under my hanging coats. A hike was not a hard sell with me. I used to beg Mum to take me to the park, any park, so that I could wander on and off of the marked trails, exploring the plants and looking for animals. She would smile when I brought back neat rocks or hauled her over to look at pretty flowers or mushrooms I had found. Or, best of all, bringing her a toad if one managed to be unlucky enough to catch my attention. She had always smiled, told me I was far too young for a familiar yet, and help me release the poor amphibian someplace safe.

I ate another blueberry, letting the tart break through the sour stomach the memories churned up. A walk would be good. Late July was not a time I should be sitting alone and listening to the thoughts sloshing around in my skull. I had hoped a familiar would give me something else to focus on, but that was proving a pointless exercise in frustration.

I retrieved my hiking boots from the tray just inside the door and leaned outside to knock the worst of the dried mud off of them, remnants from my last adventure. There had been a lot of unexpected rain, and a surplus of mud and laughter. There was nothing as fun as being caught out in a cold rain on a hot day. Boots clean, on, and tied, I grabbed my gnarled old hiking stick, a small container of blueberries to snack on, and got into the beat up old red CRV that had been a friend's work-horse of a car before it became mine. You could watch the road if you were sitting behind the driver seat and looked down. That hole was new, and I was still trying to think of ways to make a game out of its existence before I finally gave in and retired the Old Girl.

I was fond of old cars. Never pretty, but they were always full of potential. Mom used to dare me to drop coins down the hole in the front passenger floor of Dad's old Rust Bucket of a car, to make wishes. I had been too young to make note of anything else about that car, but I was fascinated with the hole in the floor.

Holes were interesting. Something was missing, something should have been there. In that way they were a tragedy. Another blueberry to coat the mouth and to hide the sudden dry taste of anxious bile. Holes were also an invitation to look, and move, through. They were opportunities.

I didn't need my morning tea-leaf augury to suggest I should pursue this opportunity. Something new, something fresh. The tart bite of blueberry in my mouth flooded the hole that was nagging at me, but it was unable to fill it.

I looked up the address for the swamp on my phone, sent it to my GPS, and started on the short, short quest to find the entrance, which happened to be a narrow drive just past a lovely, battered old sign that was quite easy to miss. I looped a long country block to come back around a second time.

On a Wednesday afternoon mine was the only car in the parking lot. That suited me just fine. I marinated myself in the insect repellent spray I concocted at the kitchen table at least twice a season, mixing up the perfect blend of herbs, oils, and intent. Once I smelled thoroughly of sharp and woodsy essential oils and I could feel the 'stay away' I had crafted settle around me, I set out through the woods.

It was one of those perfect days. The sun was out, but not too intense. There was a subtle hum of insects, but they were minding my bug spray and keeping their distance. Birds were shouting and singing, and a faint breeze was cheerful with the scent of flowers. A gorgeous day and a new place to explore. I could feel my mood bubbling with interest and excitement as I wandered along trail from the parking area.

As the wooded trail broke out into a boardwalk through open swamp, I was happy to see a rat snake curled in sun-warmed bliss around a post. "Hey big fellow. Aren't you handsome." I got as close as was polite, and then stepped a bit closer. The snake flicked an irritated tongue and unwound from the post to slip down into the swamp. Mom had always tried to remind me about serpentine personal space when I was intent on pursuing the healthy population of garter snakes that slid through her yard. But there was something fascinating about snakes. The way they moved, the gorgeous depth to their eyes. I was always excited to see them as a child.

Mom had always said my familiar would either randomly cross my path or be given to me. I waited a minute or two, just in case the snake changed his mind. A snake wouldn't be a bad familiar. My cousin had a snake, and that had worked out fine, though he wasn't the most popular at Yule. Most of my family quite preferred their familiars to be of the more traditionally mammalian variety.

It was too hot to linger out on the boardwalk. I was not a snake, to want to sit and soak in that heat. "Until next time." I was glad that no one was there to hear me talk pleasantly to the boardwalk. I knew I was getting sunburned, and decided I really needed to purchase some sort of ridiculous straw hat for these sorts of outdoors adventures. The boardwalk stretched through a sea of vegetation and open wet areas, where the air nearly hummed with insects all competing for a taste of me. I waved at a handful of turtles, apologized to far too many startled frogs, and finally reached another bit of woodland. The boardwalk deposited me onto a dirt trail, and like that I had a decision on which direction to turn. Back towards the parking lot, or off on what was labeled with a hand-written sign as the Fairy House Trail.

Now, honestly, that was no decision at all.

I turned onto the Fairy House Trail.

It was cool under the hemlocks that stood guard over the trail. They held little creations of stick and bark and stone nestled in their roots and against their trunks—the houses visitors had built for the faeries like some sort of Habitat for the Supramundane. I lingered here as I couldn't out in the sun, enjoying each merry creation and the chatter of chickadee and nuthatch. The air tingled with joyful intent and I basked in it, like the snake in the sun. Where would I have placed a little house of my own? Somewhere more appropriate than that time I had decided the ancient tangle of rosebush that my mother tended so lovingly was obviously hiding a door that would take me to where the faeries lived.

I fumbled my container of blueberries opened, popped on into my mouth to haul my attention back to the present, to the bit of woods bright with birdsong and lively with mosquitoes and where I was tall enough to have to fight my way through underbrush instead of slipping through like the bipedal weasel I had been as a child.

A bit of movement caught my eye, just a shift of shadow in the verdant underbrush, but it was something new, different, out of place. Setting my blueberries down beside the ramshackle little faery hut I had been visiting, I took slow, careful steps towards the movement. I did not want to startle whatever was hidden there beneath some spice bush, bedded down in spent trilliums.

"Hello." A greeting to let whoever it was there know a human coming close. I knew they likely smelled me, and had heard me tromping around already, but never hurt to be polite.

Ears were the first thing I saw—disproportionately large sails atop a tiny wedge-shaped head. A small cat, all bones and spotted fur, huddled there, pressed as close to the ground as she could manage. She. Most definitely a she. I saw her thin belly as she wriggled a bit to the side, trying to hide, and the exposed, full teats there. I saw the kittens a moment later. Two of them. Such little things. So still.

"Oh. Little sister."

There was a world of grief in her eyes, twisted in with fear. I knelt slowly, then lowered myself onto the trail until I was sitting, until I could lean forward and down until I was eye-to-eye with the little thing. "How can I help?"

Speaking to cats was familiar, even if this circumstance was raw and new. I could read the language of ear and tail, spine and lip. I heard misery in the shape of every muscle of her body, and something broke open in me that was sweet and sharp with summer strawberries. "I am so sorry." My voice hitched and caught on a bit of bile.

Speaking to cats was nothing new to me, but the way she uncurled from her place where she was wrapped around her loss to launch into my lap was. She was so small, her claws sharp, her stomach warm where fur was missing, where little mouths had once nuzzled. She dug claws into me, punctuation, as she purred, loud and panicked. As she meowed the 'why' carried in the angle of ear and tail over and over.

A deer fly bit into my upper arm with relish, and the little cat's stomach gurgled, interrupting and breaking us out of our little bubble of mourning. "Hey, let's go home." She needed care, even if she decided not to stay.

I stood carefully, taking the little cat up in my arms. She scrabbled briefly, trying to get back down to her loss. "Oh. Yes. Right." The kittens were not part of my Circle, but I could send them off, help them cross over, just the same. I put her down and set about my work.

I collected bark and stick and moss. Some pretty leaves. Some aster and loosestrife flowers. I built a fairy house around the little ones. Bedding out of moss and flowers, a roof of bark, walls of perfectly crooked twigs. There is a magic in making, finding and building. There is an intuition in collecting. My mother had always praised my ability at the little hedge magics, of listening to the plants and animals around me as they gave direction. I listened to the tiny remnants who had never been given a fair chance, I listened to their mother, and I listened to the forest around the swamp for what it had to offer. I listened to that bit of my mother I clung to and carried about with me and mourned. We mourned together, the cat, the forest, and I. And as we did, we built something absolutely perfect.

I set blueberries in front of the fairy house, an offering and a blessing, and a puzzle piece slipped into place without any of us properly noticing what we had done. I had found my recipe, shaped it out of the woods around us. Hazel twigs and snapped branches of oak and ash. Intent and need and an altar built around the lost kittens. Lobelia and loosestrife and moss and coltsfoot. Bark and stones and blueberries.

"Oh." I whispered, the sense of 'cat' slipping all through me like a warm hug. She found all of the holes I held on to, that little cat, sensing the need and filling it with her own. She didn't chase out what had been there. She noticed it, the hard cold edge of a grief held onto so hard it had kept cutting, allowing nothing to heal. She warmed it until it started to melt away.

"Oh." I whispered again, filled to the brim and hanging off a precipice without any idea of how to land safely, gracefully. My hand reflexively dug through my pocket, looking for the tail bite of blueberries, and then remembering we had passed them on. Given them away. Given them up.

"Grieve and release." I spoke the words carefully, careful with the shape of them, remembering the feel of my mother's hand stroking my hair as I sobbed. Grieve and release. The advice she had offered to a very young witch trying to wrap her brain around grief for the first time. There was no spell to them. They were nothing more than the wisdom of the older and wiser passed down to those still new to the world.

I offered them to the little cat, my familiar, and she offered them back. A mother mourning her children, and a child missing her mother. Puzzle pieces that fit perfectly together.

Magic was patient.

BERKANO

*T*rees groan the moment before they fall, a warning as they struggle. A startled crack of surprise and pain follows as they sway and list and then plummet with a sound like bones and hearts breaking. It is a sound that accompanies storms heavy with wind, rain, and snow — a discordant percussion section. It is a sound that flows with human growth and development, clearing way for houses and schools and swimming pools and parking lots.

There was a stand of birch trees behind our house. I grew up with them, each of us racing to get closer to the sun fastest. While my growth was marked in colorful lines and carefully recorded numbers, the trees passed various benchmarks — too short for a swing, perfect to climb, tall enough that my parents were not comfortable with my simian antics

One of the girls from the neighborhood would always come running as soon as I was out playing in the trees. She was a little towhead, and I remember reaching out and touch her hair when we were small and personal boundaries had yet to be established. I had expected it to be soft, like the kitten that my mother had recently brought home for me. It had been closer to the feel of running fingers through tall, thick spring grass, soft in its own way but not at all what I had been expecting. It had been a texture so different from my own muddy brown hair. But she would lean into my touch just like the kitten would, and that was familiar enough for my young sensibility to brush away the strange.

Looking back, I suppose I should have wondered about mundane things like why I rarely saw her mother or why we always played at my house. She was homeschooled, so I did not see her in class. She was homeschooled, a status almost mythical in its perceived freedom to my public schooled brain. I did not have the attention to question or worry or try to fit her and her family into the mold mine had sprung from. Instead, my thoughts had run wild with excitement and adventure — the pure joy of being young and having a friend whose antics and interests seemed perfectly matched with my own. We would play wild games in the trees, fierce warriors and faerie queens, climbing like monkeys and telling our stories to the trees.

"Beth! Beth!" I shouted her name as I ran, excitement and exertion pulling her name rough and thin. I dragged my prize behind me, an old macramé hammock that Mrs. Stevens, across the street, had been throwing out. I had seen it there early this morning when her husband set out the trash, and waiting for my father to be at work and my mother to be on a conference call before bolting across the street to liberate it. It was worn and discolored, but that seemed to be its only flaws. The Stevens' were just done with it. As soon as I made it out to the birch trees I called for my friend again. "Beth! Look what I found!" I doubled over, trying to ease the stitch in my side. Running immediately after a breakfast that had included both a bowl of cereal and a plate of toast was uncomfortable.

When I straightened back up, Beth was standing there, one pale eyebrow raised. "Are you OK?"

I swallowed tentatively, and since the pain in my stomach

and side was fading and breakfast did not seem inclined to make a second appearance, I smiled. "I'm good. Look what I found!" I shook out the tangle of knots and strings I had pillaged, holding one end up proudly.

"What is it?"

"It's a hammock. You know, for laying in. We can hang it out here. I was thinking I could get dad's hammer and we could put a nail in the big tree here — I think you stick it on with a nail or something like that. And it should reach to this tree..." I started to move, to pull the hammock along with me to see just how big it was.

"Nail it? To the tree?" Beth sounded upset, as if I was asking her to commit murder or something awful like that, not just put up a hammock.

I stopped, letting my arms hang with their tangle of macramé. "Beth? What's wrong?"

"Do we have to nail it in?" Her voice was quiet and faint, as if she was having to work to squeeze the words out.

She looked miserable, shoulders hunched and eyes wide. She looked like the stray dog that used to come around and dig through the trash, like she was expecting to be hit. At thirteen years old, I knew I never wanted to make her look like that again. "No. No. We can tie it. I think I know enough knots to make it work and we would just need to find a sort of branch or bulge or something to hold it..." I babbled on, trying to reassure her with enthusiastic levity. I could make this work without nailing the hammock to the tree, I was sure of it.

"Something like this, Sammy?" Beth ran her hand along a sturdy low branch on the closest tree. It was the perfect height for the hammock and we should be able to tie a rope around...

"Samantha!"

Now it was my turn to flinch as my mother's voice hit me like a well-aimed rock. I dropped the hammock, hoping she had not seen it and was just calling me in. "Beth, can you hide this for me?"

"Samantha!"

"Coming!" I threw a smile at Beth and bolted back to the house.

When I went back out that evening after dinner, once my chores were done, I burst into an excited little dance. Hanging between two of the larger birch trees was the battered hammock. Beth had tied it on, using well-placed branches to keep the ropes from sliding down. It was a little high, but I was able to kick off my flip-flops and clamber up and in and settled back with a sigh. The hammock smelled a little musty, a little like wet dog and clothes put away when they were not quite dry enough. But it was mine and it swayed gently and cradled me as I relaxed. I played with the ropes a bit with my bare toes. An ant was making a brave trip along the left side and I watched it as I swayed, listening to the chatter of robins and cardinals, the voices of neighbors.

"You like it?"

I rolled over to meet Beth's question with a broad, toothy smile. "It's perfect!"

"We didn't have to hurt the trees." Beth answered my smile with a shy one of her own.

"Want to come up?" The swaying of the hammock reached a slightly more frenetic level as Beth climbed in and we wriggled about to get comfortable.

We lay there for a good amount of time, lazy in the summer evening, listening to the neighborhood quiet down. I could hear the trees rocking and creaking gently in the slight breeze. They stretched and bent and brushed against each other as leaves rustled. It sounded like a quiet conversation, and I could almost make out words if I listened closely. I wanted to hear what they had to say, so I closed my eyes and tried my hardest to hear what the trees were whispering and muttering about. Laying there, listening to the trees, was almost enough to lull me to sleep and I opened my eyes in a fussy sort of determination to resist that soothing sense of relaxation.

The light gained the perfect gold tinge of a setting sun sifting through and bouncing off of leaves and the whine of mosquitoes became more common than bird song. After the third swat, one that left a smear of my own blood across my arm, I sat up.

"I should probably go inside soon." I stretched, rocking the hammock once more.

"Thank you for sharing your hammock." Beth sat up, trying to brace the sides of the hammock with her arms.

"You helped." I graciously acknowledged her part in today's adventure.

I spilled us both out into a giggling heap when I tried to exit the hammock. We were still trying to untangle our limbs and catch our breath when Beth's mother walked through the birches to stand beside us, mouth quirked in a smile of shared amusement.

Beth's mother was beautiful. She shared Beth's long pale hair and lively green eyes. But where Beth was still growing into her limbs and potential, her mother had blossomed years ago and had time to take raw beauty and refine it into something ethereal and elegant. She moved with the purposeful grace of a doe and her voice when she greeted us was warm and smooth as honeyed tea. "I'm sorry to interrupt."

"Ms. Bjarken."

"Momma."

"Hello Sammy." She smiled. "It is getting dark. Shouldn't you be heading back inside?"

It never struck me as odd, having someone else send me home from my own backyard. Ms. Bjarken had a quiet authority about her, not something that rose up enough to be intrusive, but just a quiet edge to her carriage that suggested she was used to being obeyed. I hugged Beth, waved to Ms. Bjarken, and went inside.

* * *

I HAD the perfect playmate in Beth as a child, and she grew into the best confidant a teen girl could ask for. She rarely had any boy problems — or worse, problems with mean cliques of school girls — to complain about, but she always listened. We replaced the hammock at least once, when it became dirty enough that my mother could not tolerate the thought of my laying in it. The second hammock was replaced by two folding cloth camp chairs when we became too big to share a hammock, but we stayed out in the birch grove at the edge of the backyard. The neighborhood grew up around us, a sprawl of new ranch style houses springing up like mushrooms in what had been an apple orchard past the birches. We stayed in the trees because there we could pretend we still had our own little world, our corner of everything that was private and quiet and *ours*.

Summers were my favorite, spent sitting in our place, listening to the song of cicadas fade and be replaced by the bright cheer of fireflies. I loved watching them fill the evening with their silent, beautiful conversations. I loved the way Beth would hold perfectly still, waiting and watching, as the fireflies came to her. Her hair was the night sky, filled with twinkling lights and I think I could have watched them forever. The still quiet of those evenings was contagious and I hated each time the spell was broken by my mother calling me in to get ready for bed. Beth would stay out there for a time — I could peek out my bedroom window and see her face lit by twinkling fireflies. My parents never made a fuss about her being there, so I never mentioned the oddity of her presence, twinkling long past when I had gone to sleep.

It was a warm evening. The air was still and heavy and

content and I loathed that I was going to disrupt the peace that hung at the end of the day. I juggled two cups of iced tea in one hand a carton of cookies in the other as I pushed the screen door shut behind me with my foot. I could see Beth's pale hair where she sat in her chair beneath the trees as I cautiously shifted my grip on both glasses and cookies. Walking slowly to keep the ice tea from sloshing over the sides of the cups, I brought my offering of snacks and refreshments. Beth helped me get everything onto the small glass top table I had pillaged yesterday from a neighbors trash pile. I had developed quite the appetite for trash night curb rummaging, bringing home my finds pleased as a cat with a plump mouse.

The iced tea, sweetened to a Southern sensibility, and the chocolate chip cookies were not quite a bribe, but I settled into my chair with anxious butterflies trying to beat their way out of my stomach. Beth relaxed into her chair, eyes half-lidded and lazy as she enjoyed my company and the pleasant evening. I hated to disturb that.

"Hey, Beth." I was proud of my voice, how it came out sounding so much more calm and confident than I felt even as my chest started to tighten up in an anxious rejection of what was happening.

"Hmmm?" Her quiet response was the low hum of insects in summer, vibrating deep in her chest and languorous.

"So I have some news." I forced the words out, as short of breath as if I had finished a marathon. So much for calm and confident.

That got a reaction out of her. There must have been some tone to my breathy attempt at casual, some sense of panicked urgency that slipped out despite my attempts to smother it. She sat up, still and alert, her pale green eyes fixed on my own. "What's going on?"

"We're moving." The words dropped with the dead weight of bitter finality. My mother had been excited about her new job

— working with a company she was enthusiastic about, a position that brought in more pay. She had delivered the announcement with a bounty of anticipation and joy and I did not have the heart to bring my own anxious misery in to shatter the news. We were moving. The taste of the words was laced with bile, the shape of them hard to form and I had to struggle not to stumble over them. I had wanted to ease into the news, to ask how Beth was doing, how her mother was, how school was. I had wanted to soothe my fears, the feeling I was abandoning her. I wanted to make sure she as OK and would be OK after I had gone.

The silence went on for longer than was comfortable. Beth just stared, expressive eyes gone flat. I fumbled to find words to fill the increasingly uncomfortable lack of any sort of response. Around us the trees sighed and whispered. "Mom says we have to get things packed up pretty quickly, get the house clean and on the market. I didn't even know she was interviewing or even looking. Had no idea this was going on. I really don't want to move…"

Beth stood, ignoring the tea and cookies I had brought as peace offerings. "I am going for a walk."

I was not invited, that was made very clear by her hard posture and blank expression. I hung my head. I could not blame her. It was pretty awful of me, as a friend, to just pop news like this on her. I would have been angry as all hell if she had pulled a similar stunt with me. Part of me was happy that she seemed mad. Part of me wanted a clean break, the hard snap of old dead wood. We were moving across the country, not just the next town over. There would be no evenings out under the trees, simply existing alongside each other. I had found my peace sitting under the birch trees with my oldest friend. I lost it there as she walked away, upset and betrayal sharp in her stiff movements, leaving me before I had the chance to properly leave her.

When I looked up again, eyes wet and head heavy, Beth was gone. I left her glass of tea there, just in case. And the cookies. I had brought them for her. It seemed wrong, somehow to pack it all back up to bring back into the house. I took my own glass in, tacking a smile on my face so I could be proud of and happy for my mother.

* * *

Work moves, it turns out, can be rather frenetic affairs. There was so much packing, deciding what to take along and what to send to Goodwill. I found myself sitting on the floor of my room, sorting clothes into two piles amidst a clutter of boxes, and realizing it had been a week since I had spent time out under the birch trees, since I had seen Beth. It seems I was starting my abandonment off with a bang. I pulled an old t-shirt on over the black cami I had been wearing and slipped out the back door. I pulled the screen closed quietly as possible behind me, unwilling to get my mother's attention and start a conversation about what I should be doing to prepare for the movers.

Our chairs and little table were still out where I had left them. Beth's glass had been long spilled and the cookies raided. There was no sign of my friend, no sign that she had been back to visit our spot any more than I had. I brushed a few leaves and a sleepy bumble bee out of my chair and sat with a thud, the material of the chair creaking under the sudden forceful impact.

"I'm sorry." I whispered. Above me the trees groaned in the slight breeze, wood stretching and bending, branches pushing along each other. A red squirrel started into an angry chatter, disturbed by my appearance after so many days gone. I watched a monarch butterfly drift by, looking for the milkweed that used to grow in the lot just passed the birch trees where there was now only the asphalt of the new road and rolled out grass lawns.

I waited for Beth, staying out through our usual after dinner meeting time when the light shifted to gold and the trees above us were alive with the song of insects and evening birds. Nothing stirred but the red squirrel, brave enough to come scavenge the remnants of cookies while I held myself still and waiting for someone who wasn't going to come. It was like losing a limb, the sudden absence of the friend I had seen almost daily for most of my life. It hurt.

A clean break, I reminded myself. I wanted a clean break. It was better this way. We would be better this way.

But tomorrow we were moving and I had wanted to say goodbye. "I'm sorry, Beth." It seemed silly to sit out there in the dark, whispering apologies to trees. But I had grown up with those trees. Beth had grown up with those trees. They had looked after us for years, providing shade and shelter and a place to play. If I could not say good bye to my friend, it felt fitting I should at least share my regrets and apologies with our trees.

I sat out there, watching the fireflies drift and dance through the dark. It looked as if they were as desolate by Beth's absence as I was. As one or two drifted my way it was impossible to hold in the tears. I stood before they could find me, before they could brush along the hair of arm as they settled to rest. I had always wanted to share firefly evenings with Beth, but the fireflies had seemed drawn to her, not me. I did not want to finally be part of their dance now that Beth was not here to share the moment with me.

I left my chair beside hers, leaving our space to be haunted by our ghosts.

* * *

IT WAS STRANGE, coming back to New York after so many years gone. I had never expected to go into teaching, not until the fifth semester of my somewhat rambling undergraduate career. I had certainly not expected to come back here, to the high school I had attended, but this time as faculty. Tomorrow I would go through and settle into my desk, make the space my own, and remember being the kid reading in the corner between classes. Today I wanted to visit the farmers market my mother used to bring me to, pulling me along behind her in a little red wagon. I wanted to walk along the orchards and remember picking apples in the fall, picking strawberries in the summer. I needed a bit of the quiet and the joy I remembered from my childhood.

That brought me up short, made me miss the moment the traffic light went from red to green. The car behind me honked and I slipped my foot from the brake to gas pedal. Childhood had been bright with fresh-picked apples, berries, and flowers that were too pretty to be called weeds carefully harvested and presented to my mother. Fresh fruit shared while perched awkwardly in a hammock, face smeared with sweet juice, smiling at Beth. I wondered if the old neighborhood would feel as much like home as I remembered without my childhood companion present. So much of growing up had been wrapped in the feel of her hand in mine.

I PULLED into a parking lot that did not feel at all familiar. Gone were the rows of apple trees and the fields of strawberries. Housing developments had sprung up in the past decade, a seemingly endless supply of them. I walked through the farmers market in a bit of a daze, wondering just where the produce was coming from now that the fields and orchards were gone. It felt surreal, coming back to a place I remembered as so comforting and quiet and finding that the speedy world that had swept me up had apparently swept through here with just as much vigor. I bought a small potted plant for my desk and got back in my car.

I wanted, more than anything, and feared an equal amount, to see what my old neighborhood looked like.

The rows of ranch houses were the same, though the land around them had been swept up into the developmental craze. The pond where I had used to collect buckets of tadpoles and little black snails was gone, replaced by a manicured water feature and fountain, the center point of the development that had apparently been named after it, Whispering Spring. I drove down the little street lined with aging trees, trying to remember just which house had been mine.

I found it, matching memory to what I saw, needing the number on the mailbox to verify it was the same place. There was a realtor's sign on the front lawn, decorated with a hopeful 'For Sale'. They had kept my mother's roses out front, a vibrant row of color all along the front yard. But there was a hole where the big pine had been, just outside my window. And I could hear a chainsaw out back, there was a large truck parked on the road out front, trailer of lawn keeping tools attached.

Trees groan as they prepare themselves to fall, a deep struggle, a warning against what was to come. They groan and sway, disoriented and in pain. I have never liked the sharp crack they make as they finally concede victory to gravity, but I was unprepared for the way they could scream. They were cutting down the stand of birches, and they were screaming as they fell.

I parked my car in the driveway, heedless of how I must look like a madwoman as I slammed the door shut behind me and bolted around the house, towards the back. I had to jump over the remains of the massive pine, bucked and ready to be firewood. I ran around the corner of the house, across perfectly manicured lawn, and stopped where the patch of forsythia my mother could never bring herself to remove had been.

The biggest of the birch trees was down, leaves still drifting down around it. I knew they were cutting them, I had been prepared to be upset at the sight. What I had not expected was to see Beth off to the side, cradling the still form of her mother in her arms, weeping. Mrs. Bjarken had always been a luminously pale woman, but now she was just pallid and still. All of the vitality had left her, leaving a cold pale shell behind. "Ms. Bjarken…" I breathed, horrified and confused.

"Can I help you?"

It was the contractor who belonged to the truck, chainsaw in hands as he paused before moving to the next tree. Did he not see the women in distress just six feet away from him? Had he managed to hit Ms. Bjarken with the tree somehow?

The lie came easily, straightening my spine and hardening my expression. I had learned over the years that if you acted like you belonged somewhere no one would ever question your right to be there. "Sir, I am a potential buyer. Do the trees have to be taken down?"

He raised a skeptical eyebrow. "We have a work order to remove this group today."

"Can you see if that can be delayed, please?" I needed him to go away, at least for a few minutes, so I could help Beth. So I could figure out why he wasn't helping Beth.

He shrugged with the philosophical ambivalence of someone who works by the hour. "I'll be right back. Phone is in the truck."

He didn't move fast enough, and I could do nothing but play the part of the impatient and displeased wife until he was around the corner and moving to the front of the house. As soon as he was out of sight I moved to Beth's side. "Beth. What is going on? What happened?"

"Sammy." Beth's face was a mess of tears. "He killed momma."

I stopped, going very still, and reassessed the scene. There was no blood, no sign of a struggle, and the man had not at all seemed like a killer, regardless of what every horror movie ever had told me about a man with a chainsaw. "How? Why?"

Beth moaned, the sound so like that of the trees flexing and bending overhead that gooseflesh sprang to life up and down my arms. "Her tree. He cut down her tree."

As a child, this would have made perfect sense. The world was still fresh and new and filled with magic when I was young and busy scraping my knees on bark as I climbed as high as I could to peek into a robin's nest. When there had been a pale young girl who always came out to visit me amongst the birch trees. As an adult, with too much experience and common sense under my belt, it was nonsensical, there was no possible connection between a felled tree and a fallen woman. Reason puts up intimidating blinders, urging us to see and think a certain way.

"You left us and he killed momma."

I blinked. Years had passed for me. A decade. So much had happened in that time, so much growing and learning and doing. For Beth, that time seemed inconsequential — there was nothing important to note between the bookends of my going and my coming back to her and her too-still mother.

"I don't understand…"

"He is going to kill us all, my whole family. We were safe, but then you moved."

She threw blame at me like I had any idea of how to catch it. I did not know how all of these strange pieces connected, the puzzle was beyond me. All I knew is that I had a couple more stolen heartbeats before the contractor was back, my deceit would be discovered, and more trees would fall.

It was a small house, but I remembered it fondly. I did not recognize the suburban landscape that had sprung up around it, but it still felt like home, the little pieces that remained. I worked fast from my little cell phone, finding the number for the realtor who had been advertised on the phone, making a call and presenting an offer that only slightly made the panic buttons fire in my brain. I had been intending on buying a house in the area, I had just thought to wait a bit, a couple years, get a feel for the market and changed neighborhoods. But the misery and panic in my old friend's eyes had put a halt to adult planning and pulled the assertive, impulsive antics of youth back to the forefront. I had no idea what was going on, but I did not want to abandon my friend a second time.

The contractor returned to grab chainsaw and safety gear and left, the realtor having contacted the seller to see if they could wait on removing the trees as a potential buyer was interested in keeping them. I was left in the backyard of the house I had grown up with, waiting on a real estate agent to walk me through a place I remembered vividly and talk about buying.

"Explain." It was a harsh demand, and Beth wilted even more in the face of it. I felt a bit of remorse, but my life had just been turned upside-down and I felt I deserved to know why.

She waved at the trees with her free hand, the other remained pressed against the side of her mother's face. "You won't believe me. Momma always said no one with blood instead of sap in their veins would believe me. We are the trees. You knew that, right? You had to have known. We have been friends for so long. So many of my cousins have died recently, cut down for houses to go up. For open bits of grass. I thought we were safe, you were looking after us. I was so scared when you left." Beth was babbling, words rushing to get free as fast as possible and stumbling all over each other in the process.

"Why couldn't the contractor see you? What do you mean you are trees?" Surely the shock of her mother's sudden death was pulling Beth's stability and sanity apart. That was understandable. But of all the things to latch onto, to think she was a tree…A niggling bit of an almost serene bit of certainty started to unfurl down deep in my stomach, a seedling reaching confidently for light, for the chance to grow. Beth made sense, if I bothered to actually listen. It started to tie everything together, placed the missing pieces into a puzzle I had not been aware I was working on.

Beth curled around her mother, pulling her closer.

"You know to listen for the voices of the trees, the way we sigh and whisper and sing. You have been listening your entire life." A tall man came around the nearest of the birch trees, seeming to appear out of a bit of heat haze and a cloud of insects.

My world was dissolving around me, pulled like bark off of a yellow birch as it came apart and pieces and shreds. Reality felt unstable, unsteady, jostled by the little sprout of epiphany surging and growing inside me. Men didn't just appear out of the afternoon sun. Women did not die because a tree was cut down. People were visible. I used to play games out in the trees when I was small, games about faeries and heroes. They had been games, the imaginings of a child allowed to read as many books as she could get her hands on, who was allowed long hours of imagining and daydreaming. Who saw faeries under every leaf and at the center of every flower? Faeries were for children.

I looked at my childhood friend, curled around the body of her mother, and started to cry as the sprout of understanding grew and came into full flower inside me. They were the tears of a child who still believed in faeries and the tears of an adult horrified by a loss. My vision blurred and I started at the feel of arms around me. I expected Beth, and tried not to flinch away from the strange man offering me comfort. His arms were strong, his skin where it brushed mine was rough and warm. I looked up at him, my vision dancing and blurred from a flood of tears.

There was some of Beth in his face, in his kind pale eyes and bleached hair. He smelled like fresh green things and musty leaves. He smelled like lazy autumn evenings curled in a hammock, listening to Beth hum. "You know about tree faeries.

You used to play at being them when you and Beth were but saplings." He smiled. "One of you was playing, the other was just pleased you wanted to be like her."

Beth sniffled, ran a hand along her mother's face. "I wanted to tell you. But…how? When we were little, it did not matter. And then you seemed to notice the strange little things about me, about mom, but you did not seem to care." Her voice quieted. "And when you were leaving, it would not have made you stay."

I pulled free just enough from who I assumed was Beth's father, reached a hand up to touch his hair as reverently as I had Beth's so often when we were small. It felt like running my hand through thick grass after a rain — soft and damp and alive. Of course I had noticed, but what did it matter to the child I had been? Her hair felt like grass, her voice when she hummed was a soothing cicada song, saplings curled to rub against her like they were cats when there was no wind around to move them. I had always known there was something secret and strange about my best friend. We camped out in the yard, but never once did I visit her house for a slumber party. We climbed trees like excited monkeys instead of heading to the mall and talked about the family of robins that nested above us every year instead of boys of movies. I had not cared that she was strange, that our friendship was unconventional. But that didn't mean I had not noticed.

Now, I let myself notice. I noticed her mother, limbs twisted like gnarled branches and a pile of curled leaves under her hair. The lines on her face were the beautiful lines that danced along the bark of a birch tree and her skin was the cool beauty of birch bark in winter sun. Beth had a lot of her mother in her face, in her luminescent white skin, in the laughter lines that curled down from the corner of her eyes. So thin, so still when she wanted to be, so silent when allowed to just sit and be. Her mouth was pressed tight to hold in her mourning and her bright green eyes were hard. She was the little tree faerie I had played with so many years ago, grown up and as weathered as I was. And just as unwilling to give in and give up.

Trees groan right before they fall, but they also groan and sigh as they bend, taking the wind and snow but not breaking. I had been a windbreak before, protecting this grove of trees with my love and attention. My attention had wandered, taken up by mundane things, by growing up.

But I had come home.

WEBS

The shadows were wrong.

They were a bit skittery around the edges, containing roiling bits of that were detached from any sort of physical anchor.

If Jesse had been in her own place, she would have called them to her and spun them like a good slick fiber until they were malleable. Would have worked them until they sat and moved as they should. Her home knew her, was willing to work with her.

This place was not interested in playing nice.

Jesse's walking stick tapped out a warning as she walked down the street and some of the shadows paused, retreating just a bit. She wasn't imposing, she was too short for that. She moved a bit stiffly, but her eyes were sharp and alert, her lips pursed.

Jesse flexed her hands, willing a bit of stiffness out of the joints as she looked at the street sign in all its battered, faded glory, eyes narrowed and daring the letters to continue shifting into something completely different and irrelevant.

Everything felt untethered, not just the shadows. Each step

felt precarious, each breath just a bit thick and unsteady. She felt lightheaded, her heart off rhythm. And the sign could not decide what it wanted to say.

That unsettled and off sensation had taken shape as movement out of the corner of her eye, wriggles of heat in the air, a bit of dust kicked up by a stray gust of wind. Borders were important things, and as she had crossed the border into this place, this town and its space, she had entered a territory that had gone wrong somehow.

The shadows were wrong, some declaring noon while others sulking into evening. There was no sense of time to hold onto. The town knew itself, but it could not keep itself straight. Internal locations seem to slip and shift.

Jesse was fascinated.

It had been quite some time since she had been called to look at something drifting so far to the side of normalcy. Soon after Main Street mutated into East Bend, and lefts shimmied to become rights, she managed to temper her curiosity with polite caution.

Ghost towns didn't gain their reputation from a mere lack of humanity. Humanity never really left a place. Their echoes and impressions stayed behind, caught in solidifying sidewalks and etched into the bark of ancient trees. The spirit of a place continued on inside its borders.

Ghost towns were not Jesse's favorite thing, but this was magic she knew. Witches had their specialties, and elders, the Crones, had worked that specialty until it became a part of them.

Jesse's heartbeat sent ripples down the threads connecting the world. All of those webs contained in all of the borders that shaped each place, the people they held—that was the magic that made Jesse's blood sing.

Ghost towns were tattered webs, but they were still there for her to learn and to clean. To calm.

* * *

IT HAD SEEMED AN EASY ASSIGNMENT.

The phone call came in the morning while she was enjoying a perfect cup of tea, staunchly trying not to bemoan another failed clairvoyant endeavor.

Jesse had been failing at reading tea leaves since she was old enough to lift her mother's mug to stare at the remains. Reading tea was not her path, but as she did make a cup every morning, it seemed a waste not to try.

The sun was shining, birds were singing, the neighbor kids were pleasantly absent, and her familiar, a metal assemblage that resembled a corvid named Egg, was making short work of her least favorite and most dented frying pan. It was a perfect sort of morning. So she had answered the phone almost cheerfully.

Andrea, the current matriarch of her scattered clan, a Witch who made magic with spreadsheets and numbers, and who found find a future in the winning lottery numbers, greeted her.

They clashed, the two of them. Politely. They always had. The high point of their relationship had been when Jesse informed everyone that she did not want the job of matriarch and would they please leave her alone with her spinning. Andrea, she had said, would do fine at the job.

Had Jesse any predictable sort of control over what the tea leaves were trying to say the morning, she would have said something unmentionable into the phone as soon as it dared ring. Or avoided it all together. Not that anyone in her family would be fooled by her evasion. There was enough witchcraft in her cousins to not only inform Andrea where Jesse was, but also predict where she would be after lunch.

Jesse was too old and canny to bother with pretending she was not home but it was never a social call with Andrea, and Jesse was still breaking in her new waking stick, the last having been shattered while working on the last assignment Andrea had given her. Her shoulder was still a bit iffy as well, but Jesse would never admit that to anyone else.

"There is something I need you to look into."

Ah. She knew that tone. Jesse smothered a sigh before it could brush the receiver and glared at the tea leaves decorating the bottom of her cup in betrayal. It was going to be another one of those conversations. She didn't need tea leaves for that revelation.

"Hello, Andrea." Her response was brisk, with a tone that usually had the power to make her grandsons check to make sure shoes were tied and flies were up, spines straightening and every curse word slinking so far into the back of their minds their mouths would be unable to accidentally loose them in her presence. "What can I do for you?"

Jesse could hear Andrea's slow, deep inhalation, could almost see her spine straightening and muscles bracing as if for conflict.

"Let me tell you about a town that has gone wrong..."

* * *

JESSE KNEW borders because hers was a magic of webs. Connections. She could test and tease the web that held every-thing together. Shift it. She had declined to serve as the head of the vast network of witches that was her family, but she sat in the middle of the familial web like an ancient and elegant spider.

Watching.

Hers was a strange and unruly magic in the eyes of her more book-formal family. A haphazard thing of intangible intent and emotion. It was a magic built of smiles between friends, lovingly tended gardens, familiar jogging and bicycle routes, the dog you always stopped to greet. People and place and connection. Webs and borders. She used that magic to look at the town.

The town was watching her back with a sentience that was sour and slipped along the skin like a slug. No one lived there anymore. They had all moved on, taken their dogs and their families and left behind all of the buildings, the infrastructure that had shaped and cradled their lives. Neglect and time worked well together. Those buildings were held together by memory more than solid construction. Jesse could see the gaps where wood had pulled away from nail and screw but still stood.

Doors creaked open, gaping enticingly as lights turned on in houses no longer connected to the grid. It was hard for Jesse to get the image of the mouth of an anglerfish out of her mind.

This was an alluring danger. A welcoming threat.

Come in, come in.

Rest your feet.

She breathed deep, closed her eyes, and told her nerves to get their act together. Andrea was right. Something was very wrong here. This place should be overrun with plants, buildings falling in on themselves as time marched on. Something was working to hold all of this together.

Jesse could almost feel it, a shivering strand in the sloppy web that had been built here. There was the tattered remains of the web of community that had cradled this place. Jesse could just feel its dust and feather sensation if she really concentrated. That was normal. That was how old houses felt. She liked to wander them when she found old places, brush along the bits of what they had been to who. The memory of why they had been important, how they had been loved.

The web holding the town together and aware was something very different. This web had been built over the old. Clumsily. It was like looking at a child's drawing of what something should be. The main idea was there, but it was distorted. Corrupted as it had been copied.

A child laughed, and Jesse smothered a shiver, sensing the laughter would only get louder the more distressed she seemed. A thick and slimy bit of web shivered through her awareness. There was something there, on the web.

Something sinister that was keeping its eye on Jesse.

There was a tension in the air, a sense of thwarted expectation buried beneath the haunting. Thwarted expectation was something Jesse knew very well.

Somewhere nearby, someone had been let down.

It tangled in the weeds and lingered like oil on asphalt. It had seeped down deep into this little town until it was as much a part of it as the rusted red wagon sitting at the end of a drive, as the tire swing shifting restlessly in a breeze of its own creation.

Let down led to resentment, and resentment had allowed something sinister to shuffle in. And that something had cobbled together a sick mimicry of the sense of place that had existed before. It stretched to the borders of the town-that-had-been.

A playful sort of menace was the mode of the afternoon, and Jesse really wanted a chance to settle everything down before whatever-it-was dropped the playful and went straight to good old fashioned nasty. Lights and doors and the laughter of children-who-had-been were a creeping horror. Jesse wanted to avoid visceral violence. She was too old for that, though she could feel the threat of aggression in her bones, like the leading edge of a storm front. It ached.

Egg clicked his beak and offered a throaty *"quork"* of advice that would have made a raven proud.

Jesse made a sound that probably passed as agreement and continued feeling out the area.

Egg was right to point out they needed to act soon. There was a pause as *something* took a moment to assess the situation and the intruder, a moment which felt uncomfortably similar to being sized up by a large predator.

Everything went completely still.

Jesse hissed in frustration before lifting and moving her hands in an intricate pattern that resembled half of a game of cat's cradle, her attention fixed on the existential and extra vicious temper tantrum that swelled and shattered the previously mischievous ambiance.

Egg dug talons into Jesse's shoulder as Jesse was forced to crouch and brace, hands continuously moving, pulling at bits of air *here*, and a snatch of wishful thinking *there*, and built a sense of safety around herself, weaving a web of security. Her mother would have winced at her form, her sister always scoffed at her style, but if Jesse was anything, she was effective when cornered.

The web that had been woven here trapped her reality behind a scrim. She knew it was there, she could just about see the edges of the town-that-was, but it was superseded by the town-that-wanted.

The ghost town was replaced by a vivid, quite cozy and out of date, place. Decades old cars traveled the road. Children played in the yard. Neighbors wearing clothing Jesse remembered from her own youth chatted near front doors. The town-that-wanted was vivid and lively and Jesse scrambled to locate any threads from the town-that-was to anchor herself with.

Jesse grabbed a bright, furious thread and followed it, finding the town-that-wanted's reality standing at the end of a driveway, her dress stunning and her hair an artistic arrangement of curls. She had a purse in one hand and three lifetimes of bitterness in her eyes. Everyone else had moved out and moved on, but she remained rooted to the spot where she considered her world to have ended.

This was the thing in the center of the web, that had built and fed the town-that-wanted.

A young woman that simmered and shimmered with so much emotion it hurt to look at.

It scalded, inside and out.

Jesse closed her eyes.

Malice hid pain. It hid hurt. It did its job so well that the hurt and the pain were smothered beneath those less savory emotions until only it remained. This web had been built so long ago, when a girl had waited for someone who never came. Promises broken were a volatile fuel, and the girl had worked with it every night. Wishing and dreaming and wanting things to be different. Demanding they be different.

And so it goes. Sloppily built out of hurt. Hurt wrapped in anger. Pain fermenting into an excellent vintage of malice as it aged. And then Jesse had come along and started poking and stoking that simmering fire of emotion until it rekindled. Until the young woman woke up again properly, pulling the town-that-wanted out of its ghostly echoes and back into full existence.

The young woman stared at Jesse.

Jesse was the intruder, a target.

She wanted to be a confidant, a shoulder. She had a winning smile, her mother had always said so, her voice light with loving exasperation as she washed Jesse's newest mess from her hands and whichever room had been unfortunate enough to contain her. She had a smile that would make angels weep and devils turn in their horns. Her magic was tentative at best, working at all the wrong times and refusing to fit into any established ritual. Her smile was the backup plan the Powers That Be had offered as consolation. She could reach into the web of things, see all the connections that made up each place, the world, *understand*, and smile.

It had been an excellent way to wiggle out of trouble as a child. It had been a way to smooth ruffled feathers as a young adult. That smile became a grimace of frustrated love as she aged. It became sharp with teeth to remind those around her that she may have entered her seventh decade but she still had bite.

Jesse smiled at the young woman, ignoring the way her wispy white hair lifted as power crackled through the web binding the town-that-wanted. She appreciated the way gooseflesh marched up and down her arms, the warning her magic was screaming at her, but she did not break eye contact with the young woman.

The young woman wasn't there, not anymore, not in any living sense. Chances were, she had passed away in that house with its perfect garden and wide windows, her face lined with resentment and eyes failing to look beyond the town she had built out of memories and a demand for a different ending. She was a bitter incarnation, a memory that refused to let go, to forgive if not forget.

Jesse had been there once, when her father had stopped stooping down and asking what new tricks his girl had learned that day, resigning himself to the fact his oldest was never going to be a skilled or powerful Witch. Her father's eyes had become dark with disappointment, and Jesse had almost wove herself into a cocoon of sorrow and defeat. She carried a bit of that web with her always. A reminder.

However, her defeat had aged differently than the young woman's hurt. Jesse had used it as fuel to do better. A bit of spiteful survival and a bit of smug pride when she crashed through expectations. She never was a conventional Witch. She was terrible at it. But she made an excellent Crone—the weight of experience hunching her spine just a bit, and digging lines, laugher and otherwise, into her face.

Jesse offered understanding, her hands slowing, but not stopping in their defensive weaving.

Egg clicked his beak, muttering quietly and eyeing the apparition.

The young woman opened her mouth and the wind howled, and Jesse lost a bit of her defense to that bit of web she had carried with her so long. It resonated with the girl, sending sympathy and similarity clattering down Jesse's bones. It was dangerous, being swamped with emotion that resonated with every particle of her personality that she had done her best to smother.

Egg bit Jesse's right ear with grumpy ferocity, then spread wings that seemed to grow far past their tangible expanse. Feathers surrounded her, and Jesse took a deep breath of warm, musty air. Egg was her partner, her familiar—all jokes aside, and all oddity forgiven.

"We make a pair, don't we?"

She smiled a crooked smile, the lines that life had given her deepening into tired creases. She was a terrible Witch, but Egg was always there to remind her that she was a good person.

It was acceptance that Jesse heard in Egg's guttural response. And it was acceptance that Jesse wove into the net she cast at the young woman standing and screaming a maelstrom of misery at the end of a driveway that had long cracked and fallen apart even if she refused to acknowledge it.

Acceptance and understanding, a smile that said, "I've been there"—Jesse picked at the bitter threads tangling through the town-that-wanted. The ghost on the drive wavered and wept, fists clenched, purse on the ground at her feet, forgotten.

"Ah, not forgotten." Jesse untangled the web the young woman had woven, brushing at the sticky mess of malice that clung to her like oil.

"You aren't forgotten. Not by me. Let's tell each other's stories, shall we?" Jesse wove a grandmother's hug around the ghost. Warm experience and understanding, and unconditional love.

"You're tired. Rest. I will look after you."

The web holding the town-that-wanted rippled as the haunt

gave up its hold, and for a heartbeat longer Jesse stood on a sidewalk beside a busy street, a hopscotch square under her left foot. A bit of wind sighed through, pulling at the image until only an abandoned collection of houses stood amidst weeds and cracked asphalt.

"I've got you," Jesse murmured to the end of the driveway.

She felt her age, the weight of the town-that-wanted resting on her shoulders. She carried her age proudly, appreciating every ding and dent life had granted her. But today she felt old, raw from the sympathy that had cut so deep and laid her bare.

Egg chuckled and muttered from his hunched position on Jesse's shoulder. Jesse reached up and ruffled feathers that had a better chance of scrubbing dirty plates than providing any sort of tactile pleasure, and smiled. They were an odd pair, but they had been proven effective time and time again.

"You've got me. I know."

* * *

"How did it go?" Andrea's smile was cautious as Jesse settled into the chair across from her. It was a busy little diner and their regular for debriefs. Just two older women out for brunch.

"I am too old for this." Jesse grumbled, fingers flowing reflexively through a quick don't-look-here and you-can't-hear-us.

"Obviously." Andrea's voice was bland. Far too bland.

Jesse scowled, taking stock of sore feet and aching back. "Can't you send Milly out on your little errands?"

"I could." Andrea cupped both hands around her coffee mug. "She would throw far too much magic at it. Probably fix whatever needed fixing, but it would be too much. Too flashy." Andrea finally met Jesse's eyes. "You know what makes you so damn important?"

"My winning sense of humor?"

"Your experience. The gum you keep in your purse alongside the small bills just in case someone needs them. Milly is a powerful young witch, and her familiar is efficient. But she has not learned how to temper that power with humanity." Andrea smiled crookedly. "Why send a young Witch to do a Crone's work? Sometimes humanity—with all of its sore knees, bad backs, and empathy—is the best tool for the job."

"Empathy is the most important tool." Jesse countered. She still had the taste of the ghost stuck in the back of her throat. Dust and hurt and anger. Jesse had a feeling it would be lingering there for some time, swirling through every mouthful of tea, catching when she tried to swallow. She had been so close to falling into a similar trap when she was young, letting pain poison everything around her. "She was a witch."

"I know."

Of course, Andrea knew. It had to have been a witch to build a web like that, even such a primitive one.

Jesse called a server over, slipping them deftly through the web of privacy covering their table. She would have pancakes today. With fruit and way too much syrup. Maybe it would, at least for a little while, wash away the dust coating her mouth and filling her throat. She would be awhile untangling emotion made newly raw from the emotions that belonged to the ghost girl, the young witchling.

As long as there had been trouble to get into, there had been Crones to help to untangle the mess. Jesse's mother had been there for her, white hair coming out of her hasty bun and glasses sliding down her nose like some sort of cartoon imitation of a witch. The powerful witches were always Crones in the old stories, in media. Jesse wished she had been there for that young Witch, to help her temper the mixing of temper and power that had led to such a vile web being woven.

Andrea cleared her throat, recalling Jesse from where her

raw emotions and memory had taken her. "Have you ever tried reading the future in coffee grounds..."

* * *

IT WAS MAIN STREET, where the house had been. Now that the street signs, in all their faded and slightly vandalized glory, refrained from shifting Jesse was able to pick her way across the cracked asphalt to the little white ranch house that had once had cheerful blue shutters and a bright front door. The roses had long since gone feral, losing their cultivated grace and form. Jesse could feel a fading echo of the young woman tangled in with those roses. She had loved them.

Jesse stood at the end of the driveway, smiled up at something only she could see and held out her hand.

"You look amazing. Let's go. You don't want to be late. Not for this."

The memory of a young woman, nails freshly painted, took her hand and the last bit of tension eased from the web of the town-that-was. Jesse felt the last bit of tension unknot from her stomach as well, though her shoulders would take a bit of time and work to find their relaxation.

Empathy. Understanding. Remembering.

A Crone's work.

Leave the flashy stuff to the young Witches.

Jesse grasped her stick and walked back to where she had left Egg with the car, hoping he had not eaten anything important.

CROW WOMAN

She was not beautiful, not by any typical aesthetic. Too often there were twigs and tangles in her hair. Too common were scratches and scars across her skin. Her voice was rough as a cat's tongue, coarse as a jay's shout. Her limbs were long and spindly, sun-toned skin and exuberance-toned muscles stretched taut over bone. All too often she forgot simple things like shoes or a shirt, seeming content to lay on dewy grass and sigh as the sun rose to warm her.

No, she was not beautiful, not to anyone who did not know her. Her eyes were too dark and wide, blinked too rarely as she tilted her head to the side and stared at whatever caught her attention. Her expression rarely softened into anything that could be considered warm or welcoming and the way she moved contained a grace, and a speed, that could shiver the fear of prey before a predator into existence.

But I knew her. I knew the way she tilted her head when she was listening, even if her eyes were flitting about, looking anywhere but at me. I knew the way she leaned in, just a bit, when she wanted company and contact, and the way she went still and straight when she would rather be left alone. I knew the graceful flow of long limbs as she danced in the rain. I knew the way her dark eyes glittered when she smiled.

And she smiled at me often.

* * *

THE REALTOR WAS A YOUNG MAN, with a broad smile that seemed to beg I find him likeable. He had shown me two houses already, pretty little things with perfect porches and pleasant little gardens out front. But they were so close to their neighbors, each house in the line along the rose near enough to the next that I might as well stay in the city.

I needed space. There was an oppressive terror to being caught in close, pressed tight against other people. There was an unpredictability to crowds that made my heart slam and stutter. My words stuttered as well, flapping and panicking around and over themselves like a flock of birds. It took me a couple tries to get my concern across, that I wanted something a bit more to the side, a bit off from what was more common and convenient. He thanked me for his time, I apologized for taking it, and I went back to the Airbnb at the edge of town that was currently serving as my base of operations.

I attracted too much overly pleasant attention as a tourist, too much bald curiosity as a potential neighbor. It was a relief to close the front door and slink over to, sink down into, the couch of the quiet house. There was comfort in the quiet. I could just hear the stray bits of evening traffic that wandered past on the street. My own thoughts were loud enough to block out anything the walls did not, caught in a loop of panic and fear and worry. This was my last best idea, my final sortie against all that mental noise of my own creation. My self-made burden that I had no idea how to discard, and thus attempted to at least alleviate the symptoms.

I tried to sketch a little on the back of a take-out menu as I sat on the couch in the fading light of the day. Nothing more than a doodle, really, the shape of a woman who I had meant to be dancing, arms spread in ecstatic exuberance. I snapped the tip of the pencil, throwing it away and pushing the menu with its aborted sketch to the far edge of the coffee table. She looked like she was bent in terror, not exultation, arms out in front of her to fend off as opposed to open to embrace.

* * *

THE FIRST TIME I saw her, I mistook her for a trick of the light, an apparition constructed by shadows and anxiety at the edge of the woods that lined the long driveway. I passed her on the long drive up to the small house, turning my head for a quick look, a confirmation, but nothing was there. The realtor, with his prepared smile and bright eyes, was waiting on the front step, else I would have stopped to make sure no one was there. But I could feel his attention on me, sharp and uncomfortable, so I continued to drive, not wanting to attract more attention than I earned as his client. Not wanting to attract the label of crazy, not someplace new. It defeated the purpose of putting myself through all of this extra anxiety and uncertainty.

I followed him in, but looked back out the door as the skin between my shoulder blades itched and wriggled, nerves dancing, warning me someone was looking. A quick look over my shoulder caught a bit of motion, what could have been a woman there standing in the drive with her head cocked to the side in curiosity. I swallowed the startled sound that tried to slip out of my mouth and turned away. I had no time for the games my brain loved to play. I was busy playing the bright young first-time home buyer, allowing a smile just as packaged as my realtors to unfold across my face as I turned back to him and shut the front door.

It was increasingly difficult to convince myself she was a

trick of the light, a trick of the shadows, a trick of my own anxious mind. She was too present, hovering at the edge of the rose garden gone wild, just visible through the broad leaves of some wild grape that had gone vining up a crooked old dogwood tree. Her eyes gleamed at me, catching the light as she turned her head to regard me from one side, then the other. I found myself looking for her as the realtor explained how there had once been flower gardens, neat little plots of vegetables, in all the wild weed and grass that had taken over the lawn. It was almost a game of hide and seek between my self and the specter, the haint, the faery. I had no other words to explain her, no other way to describe the flit of her presence at the corner of my eye, the feel of her gaze on my back.

That gaze followed me as I walked out of the house and back to my car, steady and sure, though of what I was not certain. I had little enough surety in my life I was surprised I could recognize it. It had to be something to do with that little house and its persistent haunt.

I called the realtor the next morning and made an offer.

* * *

I FOUND HER, or she found me honestly, a week later, the day I came to move into my little house, the modest Pod containing everything I cared to move with me waiting in the drive. It was cold, it was rainy, and I was trying desperately to get a key to turn in a stubborn lock to let myself into the house that had been mine for less than four hours. It had worked effortlessly for the realtor, a smiling young man who was so very earnest. The key had turned and he had gestured me in to where it smelled slightly of old potpourri, of cinnamon. There was no reason it should not work for me.

I had bought the tiny house to answer a need. It was so different from what I was used to with its bare, shoe-worn floors and peeling floral wallpaper. I bought it as a retreat, a place to hide, to provide a piece of the world that was small enough for me to fully comprehend. Instead it provided the incomprehensible as I tried to coax the door to open.

She slipped past me as I stood on the stoop, hair dripping water onto my nose. She jiggled and jostled the lock and it yielded instantly, as if sorry for its previous behavior. She let me enter before squelching in after, leaving toe prints on the old wood as she stalked forward on the balls of her feet.

My world consisted of a tiny house in the woods outside of a small town in upstate New York and a wet, skinny woman who had yet to say a word but who looked at me expectantly.

"Thank you." The words tripped out into the air, uncertain. I was well beyond my comfort zone, faced with a strange sort of stranger and a house I could not yet properly call home. Politeness was a shield, and I wielded it with desperation. I had no towels, they were packed away somewhere still. So I offered what I had on hand — thick curtains that smelled somewhat like old smoke and mildew. I held them out to her as I stood by the window, smiling awkwardly — what else does one do in this sort of situation?

It would never occur to me to strip down in front of a stranger, exposing every inch of flesh without a care. But she did, sliding out of a dress that was more a courtesy covering than proper clothing anyway, worn and ragged and scandalously short according to my sensibilities. She wriggled about in the curtain, huffing quietly and happily. I could smell the musty damp odor that accompanied her, the smell of something that has not been dry for quite some time. I wondered if her fingers and toes had gotten all pruney. I was jostled from my rather strange train of thought by fingers roughly plucking at my sodden shirt.

"Hey, wait a second..."

"Shhhhh." Her voice was the dry rattle of wind through dead

leaves as she batted my defensive hands down. "Shhhhh." It was a gentle susurration, as she pulled my wet shirt over my head, coaxed me out of my pants and wrapped me into the dry panel of the curtain.

I looked at her, all lean, uncooperative, naked angles. I looked down at myself, stripped to my skivvies and wrapped in a curtain that smelled old and misused. And I laughed. I laughed until I warmed up, until my sides hurt and my stomach tightened around the hole where dinner should be. I laughed and she smiled along with me, mouth cracked open and eyes glittering with a strange brand of humor I would learn to recognize as solely her own. She was intent and amused, dark and deliberate, and reminded me of young crows I had enjoyed watching as they explored and entertained themselves. If crows had a monarch, I imagine she would be their queen.

I laughed and my world pulled together — my little house, my musty curtains, and my crow woman with the rough voice, dark hair and darker eyes.

* * *

SHE WAS NOT beautiful in any normal way, but most definitely somehow insidiously so. She settled into my little house like she belonged there, helping me unpack boxes the next morning until we found the coffee pot, and then the coffee. Sugar was discovered lurking in the very bottom of the box of pantry items and two mugs had been scavenged from the slightly dilapidated box of dishes. The look on her face as she watched the coffee brew was amusingly endearing, the expression as she slurped in her first mouthful divine. She was beautiful in that everything seemed new and magnificent to her, from the curtains I purchased that first afternoon to the welcome mat I rolled out in front of the door.

Bit by bit she helped me make my little house into something wonderful — unpacking and organizing and being present to the point that I never questioned her right to be there. She was the unplanned element in the middle of my attempt towards control. Somehow, I did not mind. She was never invasive, intrusive — she seemed more interested in the game of making house than making a nuisance of herself.

She liked to putter. I was not at all used to being puttered around — was not used to having people around me. Not anymore. But she slid casually into and through my personal space with a quiet rustle, moving things from here to there, adjusting and designing as I moved in. I could not tell to whose preferences she was arranging knickknacks on a shelf, bowls in the cupboard. Either our tastes were so similar as to not matter or she was a rather quick study in partialities I did not realize I exhibited. My favorite mug was always clean, always waiting by the pot first thing in the morning (regardless of where I left it the night before). My shoes always made their way to the mat I had placed to the left of the front door (even if I had managed to kick them off across the house somewhere).

She pressed close in the evening when I turned on the television to start turning off my overactive brain. It wasn't a cuddle, but it was definitely a plea for contact, and it was not long before I reflexively adjusted my position upon sitting down to accommodate her angles rather than readjusting as she moved in.

I soon learned to take an attitude of wry indulgence when it came to her half-feral nature in regards to clothes. She was predictable in her negligence towards things like pants, sometimes getting half there in attending to one sock, but not the other. She would shimmy and scratch if she stayed in clothing too long, or would wriggle if she found something too confining. And those were the times she remembered clothing at all. My unplanned housemate was not at all suited to going out, heading to a restaurant or club. But that suited us both just fine. I was more inclined to paint than to plan an outing anyway.

Her disregard for social expectations extended to sleeping arrangements.

To say I was surprised the first time I woke to bony arms wrapping around me would be quite the understatement. I fumbled out of dreams and almost out of the bed before I recognized her particular chuffing laugh. "What? What are you doing?"

"Shhhhh," came the familiar response, as she reached out for me. Her dark eyes glittering in the bit of light sneaking in from outside, asking what she could not seem to find words for.

I will admit, I was as lonely as she seemed to be, and I curled back up in the bed and learned to go to sleep soothed by the sound of her regular heartbeat, her light breathing with its slight whistle of a snore. The slight weight of her arms and legs on and around me. And if she always made sure a window was open, letting in the sound of insect and amphibian and owl, I did not mind. It was infinitely more comforting than the noisemaker I had purchased ages ago at some store or another to make thunderstorms for me while I slept.

* * *

SHE STARTED A GARDEN OUT FRONT, a garden of forest flowers and creeping vines that were as wild and beautiful as she was. I planted tomatoes and peas beside them, the juxtaposition making me smile. She liked to sit out there, beside flowers that were small and purple, humming quietly with her toes in the dirt and her eyes towards the sky. I could never make out words in her voice, but the melody was calming.

Even if I did eternally worry that someone would come by and catch sight of more skin than was socially acceptable. We were outside the town proper, in the hills where houses were too small, too old to be attractive to tourists. But the hustle and bustle of the seasonal wave of visitors was close enough that I worried, occasionally, that someone would wander our way. Even if just accidentally.

I learned to have my mail delivered to a Post Office box rather than the house as she was fickle around strangers. Often she did not like them getting too close to the house itself, while other times she was inappropriately affectionate and open. Either way, it was just asking for trouble and explanations I had no way of giving.

That first time the mail had been delivered, after I had changed my address and convinced weeds and vines to relinquish their grip on the old post box at the end of the drive, my crow woman had gone still as a pointer with a scent. Her eyes had narrowed and she had started to stalk forward, movements predatory. The flowers she had been tending were forgotten, her grace slipping into something a bit more threatening, her elegance alien and monstrous. I stumbled to my feet and rushed to the end of the drive, knowing I needed to get there before her, to be handed the mail, to demonstrate there was no harm in it. At least, right then, she was wearing a sort of sundress so that was one less thing I had to distract a smiling civil servant from. Life and limb were preserved that time, but my heart took a long time to stop its stuttering, to calm. I was terrified to think of what would happen should the mail come when I was out. Or asleep. Or doing any of the myriad of other things that kept a person from sitting and watching for their mail. There being no market for 'Beware of Crow Woman' signs, a Post Office box it was to be. I did not think too long on why I was so sure things would go so very wrong. I was good with body language, and there had been a definite threat in her eyes.

I never stopped to think on why she never frightened me.

It occurred to me it was probably unhealthy, this isolated relationship I had with my crow woman, but I was content. I was happy. Which was more than I had had previously, before my little house in the woods. Before my crow woman. The warm smell of her was soothing, the thin but not at all fragile feel of her around me was comforting. Something quiet had been coaxed back to life deep in me, and she nurtured it with every casual embrace, with every harsh, happy laugh. I tended it with every mug of tea I handed her, with every evening I pulled her close before she had a chance to shift as close as she dared.

She kissed me for the first time as we sat in our garden, watching fireflies in June. Her lips were dry, her tongue darting aggressively even as her eyes were tentative. I reached around and rested my hand on the back of her head, gently holding her in place. Gently accepting. Wanting. Loving. I had come to the forest looking for something, and something magnificent from the forest had found me.

* * *

HER EYES WERE on my back when I left for town — groceries did not get delivered in a place such as this and I wanted a better liner for the shower. Comfortable enough in my own skin for the first time in so long I did not realize I was a stranger in my own town. The weird woman who lived on the hill. I did not feel eyes on me as I filled my car with gas. Never sensed how they sized me up, judging, assessing. My mind was already home, making adjustments, nesting. Curled around my crow woman.

I started drawing again for the first time in ages shortly after I learned my crow woman tasted like berries and a hint of old tea, wanting to capture the quirk of her smile, the sharpness of her laugh. I wanted her angles to slant across my paper, soft in charcoal, blended and caressed into shape with my own fingers. There, in my own little pocket at the edge of civilization, I pulled myself together on paper, reshaping myself even as I gave shape to her.

I had been an artist, once, loving nothing more than that feeling that there was nothing apart from what was unfolding on the paper in front of me. There was no awareness of self, of tools — just creation. I missed that. It was some of what had prompted me to purchase a tiny house in the middle of nowhere. I had lost something previously when my life went sour. Somewhere my ability to create had frayed. I limped along, but I was still too aware...

"Shhhh..." she whispered, wrapping her arms around me the first time I grew frustrated with the limits of pencil and paper and tore a sheet from my sketchbook. "Shhhhhh...." She soothed, pressing kisses into my hair until I calmed down, allowing myself to be frustrated without getting violent against my tools, against myself.

When she unfolded from around me, taking with her the slightly musty smell that reminded me of fall and forests and birds and her, I started a new drawing. I drew her as she stretched and lounged amidst black-eyed susans and bee balm, naked and comfortable in her skin as I never seemed to be.

Unless her skin was pressed to mine, her breath rasping in my ear. She was like putting on another set of clothes, rolling into a favorite t-shirt that had been worn to extreme comfort, perfect fit, and always smelled just ever so slightly of things loved.

I smiled, this time, as I drew. And she smiled as I worked, as she watched a bee alight on her knee for just a moment before moving on. She was my muse, my bit of forest depth and peace broken free and given life and shape. She was inspiration and she was peace and I blossomed under her attention. It was idyllic, this moving in and settling in, this discovery of my little house and all the little pieces of myself, of life, that seemed to finally fit together so effortlessly.

* * *

IDYLLS ARE ALWAYS BROKEN. Mine was disturbed by a knock at the door. I looked up, and around. My crow woman had brushed past on her way outside to play in the wind that came before the rain that had been threatening since we woke. I was less of a wet creature, preferring to stay indoors when thunder rumbled nearby. Alone and anxious as I had not been since I had driven my hatchback out to this place in the woods, I moved through the little house to answer the door.

"Hello. I hope I'm not bothering you. My car died, down the road. I just need a phone…"

He seemed awkward where I am pretty sure I looked terrified. "No. No bother." My voice was as rough as my crow woman's, harsh from disuse. We communicated in smiles and looks around here, touches and weighty glances. He was almost familiar, in that way some people from the town were familiar — faces I saw when I picked up mail and milk, part of the scenery but not part of my life. I never sought out eye contact, much less social interaction. "Would you like to come in?" The words slow and deliberate. That is what one offered, in these situations.

"Thanks, I appreciate it."

I was too comfortable in my little house, in the safety of isolation. I had never paused to consider possible danger. The danger was in hands far stronger than my own that pushed me aside as soon as the door was shut, in a body that was overwhelmingly concerned with intimidation. I was breathing too fast, too shallow, to scream. I was too terrified to do anything but freeze up as he pulled a gun. I pressed myself back against a wall (recently repainted, I remembered laughing at a dollop of pale yellow on my crow woman's cheek), trying to be as small as possible. I don't know what he could possibly want in my tiny, isolated house. I had so little of value to someone who was not myself or my crow woman. He scared me with his abrupt motions and the weapon he handled like he was familiar with it. He terrified me as he started to rifle around the living room, seeming increasingly irritated to find nothing important, expensive, special.

I was anxious, always anxious. Terrified of people, of the unknowns they carried around with them, the unknowns they represented. It had driven me away from my big apartment with the expensive furniture and my art on the walls. Away into the woods where my crow woman found me and I had started to heal. This intruder was the embodiment of late night fears, the stair or the hall making a noise when all should be silent. He was the embodiment of a fear of crowds and being crowded as he rounded on me, gun raised, wanting to know where my valuables were.

The sound of breaking glass was accompanied by the screaming of crows. A whirlwind of fury funneled into the living room from the kitchen, black wings slashing through my panic, cutting the silence.

A murder of crows — all furious shouts, jabbing beaks and scratching claws. They filled my little living room, pulled at the hair, the skin, the clothes of the man from the town. His blood splattered on my pale yellow walls as he desperately tried to protect his eyes — his interest in me, my things, forgotten as he stumbled away.

Even predators can turn prey. I watched as they scratched and jabbed at him, pecked and tore. I smelled urine and sweat as he tried to find the door in the tangle of wings and anger that wove confusion through such a small space. I cowered there, against the wall where he had left me, and watched dark feathers snap through the air, listened to the shouts and screams of the crows and was comforted. They sounded so much like my crow woman, her presence expanded to encompass an entire flock, to fill the entire space.

And in stalked my crow woman, dressed only in her long dark hair, her face painted with an anger I had never seen before. The crows quieted when she entered the room, but did not release the man, keeping flesh and clothing clutched in claw and beak. He stood still, dripping a humiliating mix of bodily fluids onto my carpet (I remembered my crow woman wiggling her toes in it in delight when it was first installed) and he stared at her in horror.

She was not beautiful, my crow woman, not to anyone but me. Her angles were harsh, her voice was rough, and her eyes at this instant contained nothing even remotely kind or human. But I had never loved her more. She brushed a hand along my arm as she passed, comforting, consoling and promising. She tilted her head to the side, eying the man from cold, cold eyes analyzing, assessing, terrorizing. This was a side of my crow woman I had never seen — a darkness and vicious edge that threatened that which had intruded into her territory, had intended harm to what was hers. Who was hers. If crows had a god, she was here standing before me, defending me. She was the dark heart of the forest stirred to anger in my defense.

"Make him go away." I whispered in a voice that was now rough from fear and embarrassment. I pressed myself against the wall, to try and smother the shaking.

She opened her mouth and blinked once, slowly, at the crows, then pointed at the intruder with a finger that was sharper than I remembered, the nail a vicious point. The crows erupted in chatter and my crow woman added her voice to theirs, slipping a vicious hiss and rattle into their shouting. Wings flapping, beaks snapping, they drove the man out my door and soon their voices faded until it was myself, the musty and musky smells of conflict, and my crow woman alone in the living room.

Her expression beckoned, eyes warming even if her face did not soften, not really, as she opened her arms.

I pushed away from the wall, stumbling the few feet that divided us and fumbling into her. I could still feel his hands, smell his breath as he shouted. I shook as she embraced me, nails like talons as she gripped me close. "Shhhh...." She huffed against my hair, nuzzling ever so slightly.

I could still smell blood in the air, could smell it somehow in her breath, beneath the mint tea that was far more familiar. I should be terrified of this creature, this murder of crows caught and hidden beneath a human skin. She was a night terror given breath and bone. But she was the force of nature that quelled my own night terrors. Her arms around me, as they were now were grounding and gentling and everything I had ever needed.

My beautiful, impossible crow woman. She was a thing of forests and sketchbooks. She was a thing of dreams and myths. She was holding me close, holding me together.

The skin on her palms was rough from working, from gardening, from being outdoors as much as she was, and her fingers were claws, but her hands soothed the shakes from my body. Her harsh voice sang calm into my ears.

Dark, sharp eyes appraised me the next morning after I showered. I breathed deep and met her gaze, water dripping from my hair to my nose. I had made a decision, standing beneath hot water, the smell of soap strong in the steam, the memory of her strength and ferocity vivid in my mind.

"I need to go to town."

A smile broke over her face, mouth gaping open as a single approving shout of a laugh shot free.

My crow woman, with the dark core that seethed beneath her laughter, made me safe. But I needed to continue the work she had allowed me to start. Now I would be strong. I would pack my purse, gather my coat, and drive in to town in my battered hatchback and file a report. I would spend some time in the café, in the library, and learn the people in the town, how they looked at me. How they looked at each other. My crow woman had taught me the trick of casual glances, subtle touches. Of learning a person so that I could taste their personality.

Maybe I would even stop by the local gallery and see if they might be willing to carry my art. The quiet of the woods and my crow woman had allowed me to start to learn myself, to heal the jagged edges that fumbling through life had sharpened. I needed to learn how to carry myself, to be comfortable in my own skin. I needed to relearn the shape of confidence as I found a new place for myself in the world. I would look up a therapist, give speaking and listening a try again. Listening had become so much easier after time with my Crow Woman. Maybe I would be better at finding the words that had always evaded me before, leaving me as baffling to each therapist as I found them to be.

That was for tomorrow. I would wander down into the mundane world of words and uncertainty tomorrow. Now, I was willing to be pulled close, to breathe in the warm, musty smell of my crow woman, to feel the peck of a kiss against my hair. Now, I would tangle limbs with my impossible, perfect crow woman and remember how to be something other than afraid.

THE WAY OF SISTERS

"She used to stand out there and caw at the crows, you know." Nana sat with me at the kitchen table. Every now and then she casually tapped me on the knees as my little legs felt the need to fidget and kick against the table legs and set the hanging leaf clanging. "She would be out there in the morning, early as anything, waking her father up, hollering at them, trying to send messages to her dead grandmother."

Ma had been a skinny girl, sticks for limbs and straw for hair. I had seen pictures on Nana's wall, sitting on display in various corners of the house. I loved to imagine her out back, shouting back at the crows as they gathered and gossiped along the branches of the old butternut tree — her posture assertive, just this side of aggressive, as she added her gossip and gab to theirs.

Nana loved to tell stories of how crows could be coaxed into carrying messages from our world to that of the spirits, stories that seemed unreal as soon as we were back home in the city. Nights visiting Nana were nights riddled with cricket song and the huffling snore of my sister in the cot beside my bed. They were nights rich with thoughts of crows moving between one world and the next with messages strung on their wings. Something as mundane as a crow gained a mysterious, mystical air up in the mountains, and they were always present — settled atop trees and phone poles, poking about in the grass. As my sister and I tussled like a pair of puppies in the front lawn over our favorite blue ball I could always hear the crows cackling right along with us.

I always felt the crows were laughing at me as they sat up in the old butternut tree, talking to each other about things I did not know, could not know, and mocking me for my lack of knowledge. I would stand out there, waiting as Grandpa gathered butternuts for us to shell on the front porch, listening to the chuckles of crows.

Maybe they knew I was the daughter of the brazen girl who used to get up each morning to join in their conversation. But I was never brave enough myself to glare up at them, puff out my chest, and let out a harsh 'caw' of my own. I was always afraid of messing it up. I was concerned I would only manage a hideous garbled message. I would end up insulting where I meant to praise the gleam of morning light on particularly well-preened feathers. In my own way, I was as strange a child as my mother — my attention and interest fixated on the crows.

If I was a strange child, my sister was unfathomable. From her first tumble from the lowest branches of the butternut tree as she tried to climb up after the crows to the time she showed me the battered old cigar box she had started to fill with feathers, my sister was some sort of sprite that had wafted out of the forest. I teased and taunted her by stealing feathers to tangle in my hair, chasing her around pretending to be a fierce Indian. My sister would run from me only until her temper snapped and her hands pulled, little fingers like talons, liberating just as much hair as feathers in her fury.

"Those are mine!" Face flushed, eyes bright and fierce, my

sister was the brave one who should be out with the dawn challenging the crows.

"Fine. Keep them." We would go our separate ways. Our stiff scrawny legs, sharp eyes, and small scowls were an amusing mockery of the crows stalking around the yard, but we never noticed the humor of the situation.

But as soon as Nana's blueberry muffins came out of the oven we crept close, drawn by warmth and familiarity and family. Butter still on lips slightly purpled with blueberry juice, we would curl up in our room and whisper our secrets to each other.

I don't know exactly when Ma's attitude toward the crows changed. In a city setting, far removed from Nana's stories and the rhythmic creak of grandpa's rocking chair, the crows were easier to ignore. I would catch them carefully observing our comings and goings from atop power lines and the walnut trees out in front of our suburban home. I tried to laugh at the gooseflesh that felt the need to march up and down my arms, at the way I felt a flush creep across my face. There was nothing malicious or malevolent about a bird.

They just were.

"Maybe they want to be us," my sister mused one morning as she lay on her belly in the living room, watching the crows out the cathedral window that let in enough light to have us sunning like cats, only half lucid in our laziness. "Maybe they want earrings and necklaces and fancy hats." She rolled onto her back, stretching with a scowl. "But that's stupid. I'd rather fly."

I bared my teeth in a slow sneer, wrinkling my nose in the disdain of the older and wiser in the face of a silly suggestion. But she never saw it, her attention caught and held by the trio of crows holding court in the yard.

One morning, sometime later when my britches got shorter as my legs got longer, after a sleepover with a middle school friend that involved very little sleeping and quite a few movies and giggled secrets, I scrambled from her parent's car and stopped. I saw the crows that were waiting for me. Seven of them. Sitting on and around the stump of a lightning-struck walnut tree. Staring at me. My whole body went shivery and nauseous. I blinked. For a moment it had not been birds standing there but tiny, bony women wearing feathers, talons for feet, staring out from masks made of bird skull and beak with something far too close to anticipation. Suddenly insecure in my own skin, I slunk from car to garage and let myself into the house as swiftly as possible.

I no longer imagined having conversations with the crows. The image of my Ma, wind pulling at her straw-blond hair as she shouted and laughed with the crows, was forever darkened into something far more forbidding. She was no longer a gangly, gawky child entertaining herself as best she could in the morning; she was no longer my beautiful and whimsical mother trying to shout messages to ancestors long gone. She was a warrior warding the spirit world away from her family.

But I grew up and moved out and into college dorms. The crows faded into nothing more than something to study in biology lectures, a bit of lore to examine in literature work-shops. Animal people belonged in the stories I wrote in class, in the books I read — they had no place on my front lawn. They were added to the mythology of my youth, sequestered some-where between a belief about the wind blowing leaves in-side-out signaling thunder and that to squish a spider would bring rain. I clung to my mundanity almost out of spite. Some sort of anachronistic sense of duty pulled me to numbers and other nonsense that entangled adult life. I needed to be the stable one, the solid one.

My sister grew to be a fey and unfathomable woman—bright-eyed and dazzling in an array of jewelry and fabrics that caught every eye she passed before, a pair of wings tattooed on her shoulder blades. She was an artist of small, glittering things with eyes always looking somewhere none of us could see, hearing voices too quiet for the rest of us to notice with her head cocked ever so slightly to the side as her lips curled into a smile.

We grew apart, as sisters often do as they grow into young women. I would watch with a fascinated lack of comprehension as she made her way through life, and reality tried its best to fumble along after her. She was as strange to me as the crows that called out to the morning, their voices heavy with secrets.

I came home for holidays, and always the crows were waiting for me, smiling and hopping — my own little court of the impossible and macabre. My sister seemed unaware of anything odd about what I had always assumed to be proper birds, seemed untouched by the apprehension that hung around me like a miasma. She was a peal of laughter, a glitter of silver and whisper of bells as she wandered barefoot room from room. I found her out in the front yard after a casual Independence Day dinner, sitting in the lawn swing, bare toes wiggling through grass green with a mild summer.

"They're beautiful."

I assumed she was talking about Ma's flowers, a mix of lilies, black eyed susans, and bachelors buttons, the butterflies and bumblebees making their way from blossom to blossom in a quiet bit of last minute industry as the day wound down. "I wish I had been here to see the lilacs blooming."

"Not the flowers. The crows."

The words, the wistful bit of worship in her voice, startled me into taking a step back, dropping out of comfortable camaraderie as I cast about for the dark spots I should have known would manage to mar the quiet evening.

I blinked again, and saw two tiny women, dragging feathers through thick grass as they hopped and laughed, heads cocked to the side, peering at us from one glittering eye, then the other. The sun gleamed on plumage that glistened with the same sickly mix of colors as oil—blues and greens with shades of yellow and purple stretching between.

Words, I could almost hear words in their chattering chuckles, their rough and rasping exhalations. Their chests heaved with a passion that had no place in a pleasant summer evening, was too feral to be familiar. And my sister tilted her head in an unconscious mimic of the crows and smiled.

The crows took to flight with pleased shouts, pulling their feather cloaks tight and jumping, flapping. My sister bent to pick up a feather that had fallen, preened it absently with her fingers.

There was something musty mucking up the mulch and mowed grass smell of the evening — an old smell, dry, not altogether unpleasant. It overpowered the flowery perfume of the garden, of my sister.

My sister.

How does one explain that slow ambling descent into something just this side of madness? It was in the tilt to my sister's head, the way she was slower to click back to the here and now, lingering in her own thoughts, caressing a silky black feather. Not madness, not really. More of an untethering from everything solid and simple. Holding her hand, it felt like trying to hold onto early morning fog — beautiful, visible, but ultimately intangible but for a ghost of sensation across the palms. A moistness, a coolness, a slight hint of *other*. She was still here, my sister, but not looking at me, never looking at us. Her eyes were on the crow-women and their glittering stares.

We snarled and spat at times, for such is the way of sisters. I grumbled at her lack of concern with the way the world goes. She hackled at my lack of understanding, but always in the end our fingers curled together and, for a few heartbeats, everything was alright and understandable until time deigned notice us once more and life carried us back into our individual concerns. She drifted back to her apartment and her cats and her art. I walked into my own home, with its coffee prepped and meals packed for work the next morning.

* * *

AND, suddenly, everything changed. There was a hole where my sister had been settled for as long as I could remember. Her presence was missing and what remained in her place was an ache so bone-deep it left me gasping. No clue, no hint, not reason why — my sister was just gone. It left me scrabbling for reason and rational thought, trying to sort out just what had happened and why I was suddenly on my own.

It was suicide, they whispered, never quite far enough that I could not hear them, the disappointment and accusation in their voices. They gave voice to a thick and often inadvertently malicious insinuation that something had been wrong with my sister, it hung heavy in their tone. The insidious idea that the death was her fault and intention slipped through every aspect of interaction, pulled at expressions and added a surly weight to conversation.

My sister with the eyes that could see things no one else could, who made magic out of everything small and smiles out of silence — I could not believe she was gone. There must have been a reason, a catalyst or instigator no one had noticed. We were blind to the things my sister had seemed to see. We were blind here as well. Perhaps it was me who went mad, who had something wrong with them, as my eyes and accusations fixated on the crows. They observed our muted walk into the small church where we held funeral services, eyes bright and interested, voices raucous in the quiet afternoon. They settled into the trees over the newly turned dirt of a fresh grave. Everywhere I looked, I was met with the cruel laughter and crooked beaky grins of the crows. They were a bitter constant and I was done ignoring them.

Nana had said the crows could carry messages to the dead. I wanted them to carry me. I needed them to carry me to my sister.

* * *

It was ever so strange, to be standing out there in the early dawn, doing things I had never been brave enough to do, not even as a child. I didn't know what to say, so I said it all.

"I know you can hear me — I know you are there. I want my sister back. You took her from me, and I want her back. I can see you, bird women, I know you, I know what you are. Take me to her."

"Claiming so much knowledge, for someone squawking about like a fledgling who wants back into the nest."

Was this the voice my sister had heard, head tilted to the side and a smile on her face? Had this throaty speech been familiar to her as my own? I wanted to be terrified but my heart was too busy with aggression to worry with fear. I wanted their voices to be harsh, a crass cackle, not be rough in all the right places like a grandparent's admonishment, and soft at the end to remind you were still loved.

But most of all I didn't want to understand them, as they settled down in the branches before me — gaunt little women pulling wings about them like shawls against the morning chill. I hadn't wanted two-way communication, not truly. But I wanted my sister, a want that was so heavy, so thick, that it hung about in my stomach like a sickness and stuck me with a ferocity that put any migraine I had ever experienced to shame.

"Please. I want her back."

"We are messengers, fledgling. We are both here and there, but we cannot give what is not ours for the taking." The beak of her mask gaped open in a grisly smile. "But that is not what you want to hear, with your sharp eyes and harsh words. What reason have you to trust the nurses who have ever been at your cradle." The beak shut with a clack, boney mask rattled.

"We can carry you, little fledgling."

"If you are brave enough."

"If you are bold enough."

"If you love enough."

"You can fly with us."

"Find your feathers."

"Yes, find your feathers!"

"Feathers!"

It was a breathless cacophony, voices demanding and daring and my first instinct was to cover my head and duck, just in case they all took to flight and sharp beaks and claws were aimed at me. But the chant, *feathers feathers feathers*, caught my attention and I scrambled from the back yard back into the house, to the spare room where my sister's things were being kept as the family tried to process what had happened.

Feathers. My sister's beloved collection, still in its battered old cigar box. It had to be in here somewhere — childish fancy hidden amidst the finery of young womanhood. Beneath a parasol and beside a pair of black boots with silver buckles sat that familiar box, a bit of red on it from that time we had stolen Ma's polish and propped our hands on it to paint our nails. It smelled of old wood and the musky vanilla of my sister's favorite hand lotion as I gripped it close, blindly navigating through a house that had never seemed so unfamiliar and back out to the yard.

"Feathers."

It was a hiss, a rattle of bone and a dying breath. The trees were filled with them, crow women hunched in their masks, claws clutching the branches, eyes glittering with anticipation.

In the stories there is always a sacrifice, but I had always assumed it would be something tangible. A token, a treasure, a life. But as I felt a precious bit of sanity slip away, the comforting and sane replaced by the shifty and surreal, I knew I had paid my dues.

No more the normal life of nine-to-five for me. My eyes were opened as I opened that cigar box and offered my sister's feathers to the crows. Offered myself to the crows and asked for wings.

A mob, a murder, they descended from the trees to crowd me with their wings and their laughter. They smelled of old places, old secrets — books that had been left on dark shelves and rooms shuttered with stale air and last breaths. I wanted to cough, to push the smell of them away from me, but they clustered close, brushed me with their fingers and feathers and I inhaled.

I inhaled as they gathered up feathers from finches, sparrows, and parrots from the pet store. I inhaled as they wove bits of a cardinal's wing into my hair, pushed turkey feathers into my hands. I inhaled with a mourning doves feather behind my ear at a jaunty angle.

I exhaled and the world streamed away with my breath.

Feathers rustled, crows called and cackled in the darkness, and I tried to feel distressed at being neither here nor there. Guided by the wings of crows, carried on wings borrowed from my sister, I was drifting from the place of the living and into the place of the dead.

The dead have no use for light and color, but the living find comfort in such things. I sought out solid ground for my feet once I grew anxious with the seemingly endless drifting and dancing along currents of air that had no source and no destination. I stood, feathers settling around me, illicit flashes of color in the light from the moon I dreamed up above me. A single point of stability in a fluid bit of nothing. No, it was something, just lacking in definition as it drifted. Half thoughts, bits of now and then, here and there, you and me. I could hear the crows, the susurration of their wings in the darkness. Gentler here, even their voices seemed smoother, natural.

Or I was merely growing more accustomed to their presence.

The dead have no need for color and light, but that does not mean they do not want it. They were drawn to me, the little moon I pulled along above me like a luminescent balloon as I walked. I could see them, flickering shyly at the corner of my eye, vanishing if I looked too hard or moved too fast. They were not used to attention, not used to motion, would pop like a soap bubble if startled.

I looked down, curious, and saw the conjured ground in the light of the little moon through my arm. "Am I dead, crows?" Impressed at my lack of inflection, holding my panic close, smothered beneath the drive to find my sister.

"How can you be alive?" They laughed and clacked, swooping around me in the darkness. "What is there for the living here?"

"Hope," I answered.

Hope, the ghosts around me sighed without breath. "Hope!" The crows repeated, tasting the word and all of its flavors as inflections.

Hope, and I felt more solid than before. I tugged my moon behind me and set out in search of my sister.

Solidity was not the benefit I had imagined. With being more defined, more alive, I became more appealing to those who had been dead the longest, those who had forgotten, perhaps, what it was to be human, or who never were to begin with. They were the hungry ones — the things you feel staring at night when you walk between rooms in the dark. They are the shadows that twist just out of sight, reach towards your back and cause gooseflesh to skitter across your skin.

The only warnings I got were the changes in the wing beats of the crows, the harsh coughs of alarm, before claws swiped close. The first one pulled something of me away — something warm that reminded me of hot cocoa on a cold night. They wanted the good parts of me, the comfortable parts that were used to being loved. The tastiest parts.

I had a small moon to give me a bit of light to huddle in, but nothing else that could be considered a weapon.

Nothing apart from my own temperament and temper. I had always been afraid of things lurking under my bed, skulking about the shadows of my home. Walking through endless, shapeless dark was the last straw.

"No."

The word wobbled at first, shivering and awkward and not at all as fierce as I had intended it to be. It was the voice of a child scared of the night and wanting their mother.

"No."

It was stronger, the voice of a girl pushing as far off the bed as possible when getting up at night to get a drink. Braver, but still anxious enough to lack power. Another swipe, and the smell of blueberries drifted away into the wavering dark.

"No." They were not allowed to have those parts, the parts warm with my sister curled around me. Those were mine. I bared my teeth, straightened my back and strode forward, pulling my moon and my murder of crows with me. Shadows and lurking things had no power over someone that failed to look over their shoulder and be frightened of them. Yes, I was solid, but I was solidly determined and the shadowy things would have to look for their meals elsewhere. I had a sister to search for.

How does one search within a place that has no here, and has never determined a there? Location was a whim — the idea of looking for something an impossible concept. Locations would not do, so I sought for impressions.

My sister was the sound of bells — the ones around her ankles on bits of string, even her laugh danced down the spine like a light chime. Her smile sparkled like a little bell, her temper rolled like a tubular bell. She was the smell of vanilla and musk — essential oils placed carefully so, shampoos sniffed before being selected. She was distracted, she was distraction.

She was a little ghost gazing up at my moon with all the joy in every world reflected in her eyes.

That was my sister. Looking ever to the bright things in the world and utterly missing the dark.

"So why?"

I didn't mean to ask that question. I meant to hug her, gather her up and take her home. Keep her in a little cigar box with a bunch of old, beloved feathers perhaps. I had not thought that part through, the care and keeping of a ghost. But I had not intended to come and inquire, my tone bordering on accusation. I did not intend on letting the bitterness of those left behind out into the not-air of the land of the dead, tainting its nonchalance with something sour.

I stood there, in the light of a moon that did not exist, the intentionally dead staring down the intentionally dead.

She looked at me, my little sister, and for the first time I allowed myself to realize I did not know her at all. I saw her, perceived her, but I had nothing to call her, not in this place where a birth name seemed so trite. Her eyes were sad in the light of the moon, an expression I seemed to remember, but could not remember acknowledging.

So I gathered her up, holding a memory of what she felt and smelt like, loving every inch of her. Remembered her snuffling snores, blueberry breath. I had flown along the wings of crows, carried like a message to the land of the dead, and I had a message to give, though I hadn't really thought of it that way.

"I love you." I whispered. Love was a bright word in the darkness. It chimed like the little bells my sister had favored, it pealed with our laughter. It danced along remembered nerve endings until I was crowded with crows, crowded away from my sister.

My sister who was left holding the invisible tether to a moon I had brought her and smiling. Really smiling. I could see it in her eyes.

I had delivered my message and the crows were taking me home.

Being again hurt. The sun was too bright, the ground too hard, the air too rough on lungs that had only been thinking about breathing. There were crows on my shoulders, preening my hair with bony fingers, soothing, crows at my feet, pulling at pant legs, begging for attention. I stood in the middle of my murder, a babe to a world that suddenly had far too many things in it, and one thing too few.

But it hurt less now, that lack. I remembered her smile.

"Feathers!" The crows chortled, gathering them up as they fell from my hair, from behind my ears, placing them carefully in the old cigar box left open from before.

My sister had found them beautiful, these boney juxtapositions of bird and woman. And I suppose they were — feathers iridescent in the light, eyes glittering with avian joy and manic avarice. There was such a liveliness to them...

They probably would not tussle in the grass with me for possession of a favorite ball, but they could be company just the same. They reminded me of her — tilt of a head, broad gaping grin, hopping dance at the pure exuberance of being.

The world was different now. Bigger.

Stranger. It was my turn to be the mad one, the one who saw the spirits sitting in corners, whistling in the wind. I had traded my life for the chance to fly a message on the wings of crows to my sister in the land of the dead, and had made it back. And I would do it again. For such is the way of sisters.

THE SHAPE OF THINGS

There was a particular cast to the sky, right before a storm. Colors were skewed just to the side of natural, light seemed to be coming through a technician's filter. Clouds could slip and sneak, leading the unwary to believe nothing was amiss—they were too flat to suggest thunder, too thin to release a deluge. But they were the scrim that would pull suddenly aside as the thunderheads gave voice all at once and too close to run from.

The birds knew, those that were left. They would stop their tottering dance on the shore, desperately trying to avoid the surf while still seeking any bit of biological matter that might be left to ingest. They would pause, almost as one, and turn their heads towards the sea. It was a look of fear, and then the air would be filled with wing beats rapid and uneven as the internal rhythm of a cardiac patient, torn and broken feathers falling just ahead of the hail.

The sky was always almost green before the hail. The color of sickly plants hoping for more sunlight. The color of duck-weed being slowly smothered by algae being poisoned by the water it required to live. I hated the color green. That shade of green. I missed waving forests of kelp, the way light gleamed on a passing leatherback turtle, flashes of fish sneaking through a maze of coral. I missed the green of new sea oats as they were sown on the dunes, flip flops kicked off tiny feet and often forgotten. So many types of green. So many vibrant types of green. Nothing like this sickly warning.

Precipitation was almost as bad as the sea itself, though I was not without my defenses. I pulled long sand-and-stone scored legs to my chest, settled my chin on my knees, and pulled my skin around me. Hunched under a span of spotted fur I looked like a stone pitted by hissing, acid-laced rain, the shadows of my posture seemed the result of crushing, poisoned hail. I watched the surf churn, scrabbling at a shoreline so battered it seemed almost cruel, if I could not hear the oceans desperate wailing.

And I wanted nothing more than to scream my own loneliness and pain back in answer. We were two parts of a whole, the sea and I. But there was nothing more than a final comfort to be found in her embrace these days, and I was not that desperate, not even something as old and irrelevant as myself—a selkie unable to swim.

I stared at my mother, hummed in an attempt to hear anything apart from the horrible pounding surf, the pounding of my heart as I yearned to swim. I should have turned inland, joined the few of us that were left in our bid for a bit of sanity and self-preservation. But I could not stand the thought of leaving our mother to suffer alone- poisoned, dying, calling out her fear and agony.

I would have missed them, had I turned inland with my sisters and brothers, had I not been sitting as I always sat, bearing witness to the death of a most ancient thing. I almost did anyway, passed them off as an illusion, a mirage.

But no…I could smell them—salty sweat, salty blood. I could hear their cries over those of my mother. I was standing before I processed the action, poised like a hound on a scent. Humans.

At sea. Stupid enough, desperate enough, to be trying a boat. They were being tossed about, clinging desperately to their battered vessel as my mother tried to buck them from her back as would an unbroken horse. They hurt her, cutting through water that was so soiled, so sick, it was a constant source of pain. They hurt her, and she was going to kill them.

It was, admittedly, not my brightest idea. But I had folded my skin around me just before I touched the edge of the surf, felt it burn. This me was made for swimming, for soothing and calming the sea. I sang the quiet songs only selkies know, coaxing, trying for even a moment of calm that would let me get to the boat, let me guide it to shore before the poison killing my mother ate away at my skin.

She heard me, my mother, and paused with a mighty gasp of wind and wave. It was the wavering inhalation that came before an outburst too powerful to be suppressed, I sensed how the waters gathered, how the currents shifted, and did what I could with the magic I had.

Selkies were made for enticing. I bobbed there a moment, just out of reach, brown eyes wide and adoring. Encouraging. I made sure they could see me, I threw every bit of glamor I had to make myself the most appealing thing those humans had ever seen. I sang out the siren calls of my southern sisters—using them to coax to safety as opposed to destruction. And the boat turned, slowly cutting through the returning furor of the ocean to follow me to the skeleton of a pier. A safe place for them to cast a rope, to tie, to clamber up and away from the surging riptide. A place for me to guide them out of the sputtering rain and into the old building with its battered but mostly intact roof, ancient soda machines and a game table.

My skin over my shoulders like some manner of primitive cloak they could not help but recognize me—once a seal, now a naked, somewhat scrawny man. A selkie. There was a chance I could be slaughtered for my skin and the protection it offered against the poisoned rain, but they looked too exhausted, too damaged, to offer much of a threat. And they had a wee one. I reached without thinking, taking the toddler from his mother's exhausted, rain-burned arms, whispering and conjuring, singing poison ingested from crying in the rain out of his blood. It slithered like tar from the corners of his eyes, tracked down his face like tears until I wiped it away.

"I am Morgan." I was surprised at how clumsy my voice was, unused to the shape of my own name, how round it was, open and inviting. "I saw your boat."

"Thank you. We were…"

"We were fucking terrified." Her mate did not seem to harbor any of the tentative attitude toward me that she did. He ran a hand through the uneven clumps of wet hair that clung to his scalp, wincing a bit as the wetness burned. "Didn't think we would make it to shore, that storm coming out of nowhere like it did. Like they do."

I could taste the storm in the back of my throat, bitter and angry and unwilling to wind down. Male selkies breathed storm winds. Our hearts beat to thunder. But these storms frightened even me. "This is a particularly bad one. I could hear it when it was born, far out over the waves, so unhappy…"

We stood there, again awkwardly aware of things different between us, things of blood and bone. Of seal skins and selkie songs. But we shared a very solid need to be indoors as the wind began to howl and the rain really started to come down. "It isn't much, but this has served as a sort of home to me—I am happy to share it for as long as you need."

"I am Josiah. My wife is Marilyn. Our son is Aaron. Thank you for the shelter."

* * *

SHELTER WAS EASY. Realizing that humans would require bedding and other comforts was hard—I was used to rolling into my skin, curling up seal-stoic against the elements. Had there been another selkie to see me dashing from abandoned human home to abandoned human home, my skin held over my head like nothing more than a strange umbrella I am sure I would have been embarrassed. As it was I pretended to ignore the way Marilyn almost laughed. And she tried to ignore the fact I was not human. But I found blankets that were not too mildewed in what had once been a rather magnificent vacation home, a few changes of clothes that should fit. A set of blocks that had once been used to build sandcastles. The beach was not safe, but Aaron could manipulate them indoors.

I helped them build a nest of human castoffs in the corner of the pier house. My house. I grew used to the way Marilyn sang quietly when it stormed loudest, when she pieced together a meal out of whatever Josiah or I brought in. I grew comfortable with the feel of them around me, never silent, all rustles and breaths and footsteps. They were islanders, originally—holdouts after most of their community had fled, taking their chances atop the poisoned waters as opposed to watching the waves slowly eat away at the land offering them some measure of protection. They had been proud, refusing to leave. But a baby had changed everything and as the waves cut closer with every season they had made the decision to follow the path their community had chosen earlier, active attempt over a passive resignation to their fate.

I enjoyed the shape of their names in conversation—the breathy, bemused resignation of Josiah, the shy exhalation of Marilyn and the broad joy of Aaron as he grew. I grew to love the smell of them—salty like the sea never was anymore. The light salt of their sweat was omnipresent, almost soothing, but it caught my attention, my breath, when Marilyn wept one morning. The salt of her tears was so sharp to my nose it hurt. It *hurt*.

I was next to her, brushing each precious bit of salt water off of her face with an intensity I knew frightened her, but I could do nothing to stop myself, even as I licked my fingers clear of her tears, something that had withered long ago deep inside me swelling. I chased after it, song rumbling deep in my chest, a hunters croon. I swept her up in it, my touch as rough as the waters below as I swept her terror away. This was not the slow seduction of a selkie male in the moonlight. This had the hard edge of survival to it. I called to her, to the soft corners of humanity that were so easily edged in salt, and lapped up everything she offered.

"Morgan."

A human male, interrupting. The waters below raged in response to the pounding of my pulse, beating at the ancient pier.

It has been written into every selkie story ever told—we are a tragedy. There are no happy endings with seal wives, to be found in the arms of a seal husband. It is a fine line we straddle between domesticated and savage, we live in that liminal space between sea and shore. And in this battered world that line had been blurred so badly.

Pier shifted, the pounding of my magic having accelerated the damage of the acidic sea. The poisoned waters raged and everything shifted. Marilyn screamed, losing her footing as the world slid to the left. Josiah scrambled for his mate, a wordless shout snapping through the creaking and cracking of the pier.

I remember the pier giving one final, grateful groan as the acidic poison of the ocean finally won and it was able to start to slide to its rest. Marilyn and Josiah were on the other side of the building, clinging to each other, trying not to slip away and out. A crack opened in the floor between us as the shifting supports tore at the building. Aaron wailed, the sharp shape of his terror driving me to evaluate the situation. To move. I took Aaron in my arms and fled my home.

I did not watch the final splash of the pier house. I did not take the burden of its death, the deaths of its inhabitants, onto my shoulders. The world was a bit too broken for anyone to take responsibility for events such as this, tragedies such as these. It was not in the nature of a selkie anyway. We mourn, we grieve, but we do not suffer from an overabundance of guilt. That is a human condition. Before the waters went foul, my experience of humanity began and ended with soft smiles and touches in the moonlight—carefully cunning gestures, the slip of skin against skin and soft sounds of surprise and delight. Now it expanded to include the howling of a small body left to become too hungry, too thirsty, too tired, too dirty.

I traveled away from the sea, away from my long vigil at my Mother's deathbed, my attention now on caring for this demanding, disastrously fragile, little creature I had taken responsibility for. He suckled at my fingers as if hoping they would produce more than a sticky sort of mud as saliva mixed with whatever had soiled me most recently. It was difficult to locate creatures to milk, and I fear my little human grew on a rather eclectic diet—meat that was too tired or worn to put up much of a fight, inland plants I had no business determining the edibility of. But grow he did. He grew curious and vocal and gangly and swift. He wanted to know the words for all the things we saw, and some of the things he saw only traces of.

He never thought it strange that I would stop and stare at the sky sometimes, just before the birds would pause in what-ever they were doing and then take to frantic wing. He would simply start looking about for someplace safe, some sort of shelter for his vulnerable body. Somewhere to pass the time while it rained and I rolled up in my sealskin and lay nearby. The erratic, vindictive weather was not alien to him. Neither was a selkie.

He gave me back my words, reminding me of the shape and feel of them, the way some of them tickled, some of them hurt.

He reminded me of family, of sitting with seal maidens and selkie men on rocky shores and laughing through philosophy and terrible poetry. He taught me how wide the word loneliness could shape through one's spirit, even while a bright young human chittered and chattered an accompaniment to the rain just to the left.

"Aaron." His name was wide in the middle, a smiling shape that opened and closed on a promise and a smirk. He cocked his head at me from where he lay in a nest of leaf mulch, warm with decay, smelling like autumn used to. "Aaron, are you lonely?"

"How?" His sentences were short, clipped and concise as someone far older, as the taciturn selkie that served as parent and friend. "I am not alone."

How to explain the feel of loneliness—the narrow shape of detachment, the slippery fear of drifting? How to explain the taste of loneliness to a human child who did not know schoolyards and malls and choirs and drum circles? How to explain the way it was worms of the spirit, eating away at intangibles until all the parts that mattered were as tattered as old lace?

How to explain the horribly slow death of a selkie away from his family and his sea, how a small human, even one as exceptional as one's current company, could not slow the bleed from this wound?

That was not the talk to have with a child. I huffed, rolling tight into my skin until there was nothing there but a seal to curl close to the boy. Seals have no use for words. Small boys take comfort in contact.

* * *

I DON'T THINK I quite noticed when Aaron stopped being small, when it was two men who wandered through stunted woodlands and battered fields in search of water that was safe enough to drink, things that were alive enough to eat. But his voice deepened into a thunderous boom when he laughed, mouth wide, expression uninhibited by the concern of what others might think. He was a wild thing—expressive, uninhibited, curious. He was as close to fae as I have ever seen a human be, and I suppose it should have pleased me, this wonderful child of mine.

He did please me, with his broad smiles full of contentment with a situation I cannot conceive of anyone, anything, else being content with. He coaxed smiles out of me—soft expressions that were so unfamiliar, almost uncomfortable, but ones I enjoyed. Even as we slipped through broken down buildings, stepping over rubble and bits of organic matter we chose not to think too deeply about, or as we trudged through swaths of dead grass, around the edges of swamps that smelled of chemicals more than rot, Aaron shared secrets and smiles with me. Smiles I found myself returning more and more often as time moved on.

I was smiling when they found me, a group of humans far less domesticated than my Aaron. Their bodies scarred and battered with burns, skin hanging to bone out of sheer stubborn determination. So emaciated, so angry. So aware of what I was. I was glad my Aaron was foraging, that we were apart for this time—I did not want him to be hurt. I did not want him to see me hurt them.

For I may be old, missing my family and far past when I would rather be taking my last swim in my Mother, but I am a *selkie*. The thunder that accompanied the way I bared my teeth would bring Aaron running, the way the clouds gathered through a previously clear sky would have him worried. But the rain was not meant for him. The burning of the rain, the scorching death of the lightning—those were meant for the ones who were after my skin.

"Morgan!"

The humans fought with tooth and nail, the weapons left to

them in this battered remnant of the world they remembered, the world they had broken so far past repair. They tore at my flesh, bled me even as my rains burned them and our voices mixed in cried of furious pain that were indistinguishable once uttered. My skin my skin they were going to take my skin... I could feel the rains burn as my skin was pulled to and fro from where I had it over my head and shoulders, down my back.

"Morgan!"

My Aaron, face red and blistered and not at all smiling. He pulled a human from me, not even seeming to care as he snapped its neck with the same practiced ease he had snapped the bones of prey animals we had stumbled across. My Aaron, damaged by my killing rain, and not at all human as he fought to defend the only family he had. So fae, so feral, and for a moment I was horrified at what I had raised.

And then I was honored. Something settled into those worm tortured, lace-holed parts of me, warm and for the first time in so very long content. At the end of a slaughter, bleeding and blistered, as I sang the storms away, I finally curled myself around the concept of family. After so very long, I had family. Aaron looked up at me, blood slipping down one cheek. "Morgan. I found water. Clean water."

Water. My mouth split wide into a smile and I began to laugh.

* * *

WATER. For growing vegetation that could sustain life. For drinking. For swimming. Clean water was the key, the thing that had been missing for so very long. Aaron led me, the both of us limping and leaning on the other, to a system of caves, down deep where plants glowed and fish did not even bother with eyes. Fish. Plants. My pulse battered at my veins with excitement. Anticipation.

There was water indeed. An entire underground lake lit by bioluminescence. The air was fresh in a way I had never anticipated, so far underground. Clean. The first time a bit of moisture dripped from the unseen ceiling and landed on my cheek I flinched, and then let the sheer wonder of the sensation, the lack of pain, swell within me. I caught a motion in the waters and I shivered, standing still as a hound on point, sensing something that had been missing at the edges of my awareness for so long—there were selkies in the water. I wanted…I wanted with an intensity that was terrifying to join my sisters and brothers. To introduce my son.

My son. Blistered from rain, hanging awkwardly back and watching, waiting to see what I would do. I could watch every emotion chase across his face, I could have tasted it in the one tear tracing down a cheek had I been inclined to sample it like the rare vintage it was. But I did not need to. I understood human's enough. I understood loneliness enough. My Aaron was waiting to see if I was going to slip into that water, a seal, and never slip back out. My Aaron was wondering what it would be like to be an orphan.

Selkies are tragedies. We always have been, always will be. As the world repairs herself we will be down in these caves, in this water, writing new tragedies as humans stumble across us. Aaron was my tragedy. I could still remember the shape of Marilyn's smile, the way Josiah's name stretched and shaped my mouth. Selkies would always be tragedies but, perhaps, for this one time, the tragedy could be my own.

I slipped my skin off my shoulders, stepped back and wrapped my arms around Aaron in a hug, pressing flesh to flesh, burns to burns. I pulled my skin up and around his shoulders, pressing a kiss to his cheek. "Aaron." The shape of his name was a smile, a smirk and a promise at the end. His name was a promise. I wanted to promise him so much. "My Aaron."

I am no selkie maid to lose her skin on a moonlit beach, to

remain captive as a human until I win it back. But this thing I would give freely—my skin, my magic. I wrapped it tight around Aaron, watched his eyes go wide, those eyes so wide in the face of the new-made harbor seal that stood still and awkward on the stone floor. "My little selkie."

I know well the pulse of tides through the blood, the urge to wet every inch of the body and roll weightless in the embrace of a body of water, the pure joy of being. I watched as a human heart stretched to accommodate so much more than it had ever anticipated. My heart would always call to my Mother the sea and that call burned harsh with every breath, but here, as my Aaron felt everything new and the whiskers on his face gave an excited quiver I knew that particular sickness had not slipped into him along with my magic. He could be content deep in the earth, held secure in the arms of a different Mother, submerged in Her secret pools.

I stepped back, wrapped my arms around myself, feeling exposed in a way that had nothing to do with nudity, but strangely comfortable. "Go on. Meet your sisters and brothers. Meet your family." It had never been about me, none of this. It had always been about a small vulnerable baby crying in his mother's arms, so like the crying of a seal pup who had lost sight of its mother. It had always been about one human in the middle of a world that way beyond noticing the little things, beyond caring. I had been beyond caring, and now I was near to bursting with deep contentment. This new selkie, these new selkies—I could taste their newness in the air, could see it in the brightness of their eyes, eyes so unlike mine—they would survive.

How many others had done as I just had? How many human children had cried out, only to be taken up in the arms of seal maids, of selkie men, raised as wild and wonderful things, and finally given that greatest thing a selkie had to give? Selkies were tragedies, salt of the sea and salt of tears. Always wanting something just out of reach, on the next shore. Always reaching.

But this was a new beginning, a bit of a gleam on the horizon. These were new selkies, and they were free to make their own story, their own magic.

I walked away, making my way back out of the caves as Aaron slid into the water, graceful as any selkie born. I left those young and joyous seal folk behind in their glowing cave full of blind fish and crawling things, that cave so full of life. I walked back out into a world that had died so long ago and for once thought not of death but of a potential recovery. The chance was in the gleaming eyes of a small herd of seal folk, in the hope that curled warm through my stomach I walked, finally towards the embrace of my Mother. My mouth shaped words I had wanted to say for so very long, testing the shape of them against the warmth in my stomach, fascinated with how well they fit. "I'm coming home."

EMPTY SWING SETS

I used to keep ducks. They were the happiest creatures I have ever met and were a delight to have on the farm. With their constant chatter, tail wagging, and paddling about in the cheap plastic pool I had set up for them. Pool cleaning days were the best. The ducks were ecstatic with fresh water and played and bobbed and chattered with excitement. I loved those idiots. I loved them to the second I butchered them and tried to convince myself the gritty dust of the dead corn field across the road was the reason for my tears. Hard to keep the duck pond full when I was worried about having water to drink.

Honestly, zombies would have been easier. We were primed for that. We used to all joke about zombie defenses and preparation. About who would most definitely end up as zombie food first. Our media had been utterly saturated with explorations of how we would suffer but ultimately survive the zombie horror. Ok, sometimes those stories were not quite as optimistic as all that, and I am sure the dog died in at least one of them, but it was something that always seemed manageable. We could get over it and get on with things.

A bit harder to do when we had busted the planet bad enough that being eaten by a zombie really seemed the better outcome.

That's not to say we didn't also have a helluva lot of 'we sure fucked the environment' media at our disposal. Those disaster films were pretty popular. But those definitely had a sort of rose colored glasses appeal to them. Plucky heroes always won. Found the oasis. Worked together. Figured out the science. Just plain yeeted us all out to another planet to destroy like the bipedal locusts we were.

Being stuck here on Earth, eating the grit the wind threw at me and wondering when I was going to manage to sneak in a quick shower, made me almost wistful for those movies with their triumphant end credits. Their themes of human cooperation and ingenuity. It would be better than standing here with an old hay fork trying to fight off the feral farm dog that really wanted to get at my hens.

The hens were questionably worth defending. It had been too hot for too long, too dry, and they weren't really laying. Or getting enough to eat. But they were mine, dammit. Angie had wanted chickens so badly, and it had been hard to deny that little girl anything.

There was a collar on the dog, and probably a tag, but it was a lean thing, and desperate to get to my girls. It had no people looking after it who would miss it. It was wary of my hay fork, but also very hungry.

One of my idiot roosters got past me and the fork, tiny rooster brain programmed to attack, to defend his flock. "Rock! No!" He didn't stand a chance against the dog. Rock got some hits in before the dog grabbed him and shook once.

"C'mon. Get. Go away. Fuck off." Shouting at a dog that was more desperation than domestic. Useless. But the dog had its prize, and it was not worth tangling with me to try for more. Rock had been a pretty rooster, and good with the girls.

I would miss his stupid need to attack anything and everything.

I only had two roosters left. Thankfully they were in the gentleman's quarters, a stupid little coop I had cobbled together out of scraps of the old garage. It kept them out of trouble, and I only lost one at a time when things like this happened.

"Can you guys believe roosters were once trash?" I asked the hens, keeping my voice quiet and conversational, moving slowly around them and hoping they would settle back down in response. I needed the roosters and their homicidal enthusiasm to help keep the flock together and in one piece. Hopefully one of the broody idiots would hatch out a useful mix of layers and fighters this season, help replenish both populations.

Thunder rumbled in the distance. Excellent. First a feral dog and now a storm. I swore we weren't due for more violent weather yet. I hadn't done any of the preparation for the far-too-short rainy season yet. Season. More like a week of catch what you can and hope its enough to last. "I guess we are checking the collection system today instead of tomorrow." I still chattered to Angie as if she was following like an eager puppy, wanting to help with the chores.

The rains, when they came, collected into the series of pipes that ran to a cistern. My washing and bathing water. Water for the garden when it could be spared. I checked the pipes to make sure nothing had come free or cracked since the last good storm. I had only had the property for about a year before things got so dry. They called it "Global Warming" when I was a kid, probably because "Global Desiccation" was a harder sell. I remembered sitting and staring at the well that came with the home, wondering how deep it was, how safe I was. So far so good at least. Content that everything looked secure, I made my way down the cracked old road to the playground.

The sprawling building set next to the playground had been a school about a decade ago, before things went a little squirrelly with the weather and humanity's lunge toward every person for themself. The last decade had been a lively demonstration of how brutal people could be when the rules tidying things up came apart at the seams. It was good to have a farm in the middle of nowhere, with a bonus abandoned school property as a buffer. People passed through the school itself every now and then, resting, plotting, but they always moved on. There was very little here, and what there was I was quite capable of defending.

The empty swing sets were the worst. There should have been a mad whirl of kids out here at least once a day. There should be shouting and screaming and laughing. Angie used to insist I push her on the swing, giving her height and speed a head start. At least she had learned not to laugh and squeal, to sit on her joy.

Hush now.

Hush.

I should be sitting next to Angie, shaking my head as she played on the swings, mouth open in silent joy. Instead I sat myself on a swing and stared out at the clouds. It had been a while since the last rain and the water would feel good, as long as the weather did not take a turn towards too violent.

I had played on this playground as a kid, chasing my sisters across the monkey bars, pushing them on the swings. The red paint on the slide had been vibrant. The rubber seats of the swings had been pliable and new. The world had not gone to utter shit yet. Angie had been so much like my little sisters. The paint had been worn and there were only a couple swings worth playing on, but she had loved those stolen moments of being a kid. I had loved seeing her be a kid. It helped me forget the look in her eyes the day she had turned up like a stray cat. I stared out at the clouds, lost in thought.

"Hello?"

"Fuck!" Surprised and a good bit alarmed I turned, almost

falling out of my swing. "The hell?" My fight or flight response was apparently as well developed at that of my roosters. I snapped my gaze around the small playground, looking for the intruder.

I tried to stuff all of that adrenaline back into its box. A pair of kids, probably somewhere in their early teens, stood awkwardly by the scratched and faded slide. They had the same hungry look the farm dog had had, but with none of the aggression.

I was going to have to break into the strategic bean reserve.

The look I gave the storm was a bit more considering than before. Refilling the rain storage would be useful as well.

"Sorry. Hello. Who are you?" They looked miserable standing there, both of them, and neither of them seemed willing to talk first. "Shit, I am just bad at this. I am Jesse. You are sort of wandering through my place. Not that I mind, honest, I just wasn't expecting anyone." Especially not anyone I wasn't going to have to fight off, at least. "You guys look fucking knackered."

One of the kids almost smiled at that. "My name is Anne. This is Kelley."

"Hey Anne. Hey Kelley. Have a seat." I tried to shake off sublimely rusty manners. The playground, the swing set, wasn't mine, per se. But it was close enough to the house I lived in and a bit of surreal hospitality seemed appropriate. They were awkward and shy, but they settled into the cracked and creaking swings next to me and we all sat in a somewhat uncomfortable, unfamiliar silence.

Kids. Who'd have thought. I was a nice, safe thirty. Too old for the gangs that wandered looking for lively young labor to scoop up and sell off. Seriously, zombies would have been easier. I still had trouble wrapping my head around sane, normal humans stealing kids, selling kids, killing families. Zombies were simple honest destruction. There really was no malice in it. These Stoats, as they were called, kidnapped, stole, killed and understood what they were doing. Fuckers.

Don't go outside, the Stoats will get you.

Don't be too loud, the Stoats will find you.

Hush now.

There hadn't been any kids in the area for ages. Not since Angie. Long enough for the playground to feel like a relic, an artifact of a much more optimistic time. Kids were kept hidden and quiet if you wanted to keep them. The empty swings seemed to mourn as they sat still in the evenings. But here we were. My adult self and two actual kids, sitting on some swings. My stomach gave an acidic, anxious lurch.

We were about to be sitting in the rain. The first drop fell cold and heavy. I hoped it was going to be one of the big, wet storms. Good for the water supply, bad for physical comfort. I hauled myself out of the old swing.

"Alright, folks. Let's get someplace dry, yeah?" The space between my shoulder blades was crawling. I felt incredibly vulnerable sitting there with the kids where Stoats could find us. Girls were such tempting targets. They would not be worth much for labor, but with a population in decline, well…It was an abhorrent line of thought, and the reality of their situation was a kick to the gut.

Anne and Kelley didn't move, their faces a study in distrust and indecision.

"So, just to be clear, I don't traffic in kids. I know you have no reason to trust me, but you are the ones who walked out of wherever the hell you came from and said hello first. So you can either sit here in the rain and see if the Stoats do find you, or you can follow the crazy lady to her house and see if there is any shitty coffee left."

"We don't drink coffee."

"Today is a good day to start. You coming?" Being left alone seemed a worse gamble than coming with me. Anne and Kelley both nodded and stood.

We went the long way through the woods. Poison ivy and ticks were the easier threats. There hadn't been any Stoat activity here in ages — we were too rural and spread out to be worth it — but passing by a neighbor with children in tow was a gamble I was not willing to take. There were no rules anymore, no sense of community or connection. If a neighbor felt they would benefit from selling us out, they would.

My house wasn't anything fancy or large, but thought had gone into its construction, something I was eternally grateful for in this battered and worn-out world we had. It sat sheltered by an earthen berm and was covered in a fascinating tangle of old solar arrays that I worked to keep up and running as much as I could. There were a couple panels on the highest part of the roof that were nothing more than interesting artifacts at this point. The house was in a clearing, so all of that solar was actually useful, down to the piping the original builders had added for solar powered hot water. Sometimes just sort of tepid water, but it was better than nothing and the system had some life in it yet. I hadn't been a prepper when I decided to buy the place, but all of those interesting additions had paid off. The large windows that generated passive solar on the south side of the house were amazing in the winter but definitely would not help me survive a zombie apocalypse. I had gambled on 'humans fuck the climate up past redemption because we are terrible like that' over 'miserable zombie plague' and turns out I had been right.

The house was far enough from the road, and I had let the old rambling dirt driveway get properly overgrown, that we wouldn't be seen by anyone walking the cracked asphalt of the road as we came out of the woods, through the old goat pasture, and to the berm-sheltered front door.

One of the chickens spooked as we got close, flapping and

squawking madly in its attempt to get past us. The chicken spooked the girls, who added to the noise with squeals of their own.

"Oh, c'mon. You stupid muppet of a chicken." I moved about an inch to the left, which was apparently all the bird needed. She took her noise with her, and I hoped anything drawn to the noise would follow. It was a good thing there were so many feral chicken populations around these days. The sound of a rooster, panicked hen, or hen becoming someone's dinner, was at least as common as the shout of a jay.

"Yeah, sorry about that."

I turned at a strange, muffled sound, and saw Kelley with a hand pressed to her face, eyes wide. She was trying to smother laughter, and looked as surprised by the emotion as I was once, I recognized it. Laughter. I had a terrible sense of humor and had developed some affectionately interesting ways to swear, but it had been a long time since there had been honest, simple laughter.

I grinned. I grinned until my face hurt, until I had coaxed a similar expression to life on Anne's face.

Just three normal people standing in the rain, laughing at a chicken.

"I have towels inside...and some dry clothes if you don't mind things that are too big."

"I like being dry." Anne pushed wet hair out of her face.

"We can make that happen."

The house wasn't much—weird open plan on the first floor, couple of bedrooms with a Jack and Jill bath between. The second floor was mostly storage and the small bed and bath that I preferred. I had repaired a lot of the plumbing recently after a winter freeze snuck in past old insulation. Now the solar water heater plumbed that shower, more useful than trying to heat enough for the tub. That got the old timey haul hot buckets treatment since the old hot water heater had crapped out a couple years ago.

Which is what I did for the girls. There was an old maple boiler that I had learned worked excellently for heating water for the tub. I ran the buckets and the girls each took a turn in the hot, and increasingly grubby, water. No point getting into clean, dry clothes that state they had been in.

They were dirty, that sort of caked in staining the skin sort of dirty that came from a long haul between bathing. Hair was tangled. clothes had seen much better days. Kids were either running or had nowhere they properly belonged. I took a quick walk up the driveway while they were in the bathroom to make sure the hidden chime around front was still working. After it blinked a nice reassuring red as I walked back and forth a few times I made my way back inside. I hated being surprised, and now I couldn't afford to be.

My money was on "they were on the run."

I turned on the stove and started to boil water to cook some beans. Times like these I thanked past me for investing in that battery system for the solar. At least we got a lot of sun to keep the batteries filled these days.

The girls joined me in the kitchen as I was rinsing the second round of gross foam off of the beans. "Everyone cool with vegetable bean soup?"

I USED to really enjoy sitting around a campfire, maybe with some quiet music playing from someone's phone, chattering about everything and nothing. Just enjoying the company and the space. I would have loved to get a fire going in the woods for the girls, but I was unwilling to be that obvious. Tonight, by the grace of battery backup, we had bean soup, bread toasted so the little bit of stiff stale was hidden, and cups of mint tea made from last year's garden as we sat around my battered kitchen table. Well, they had tea. I was slogging through cold old coffee, unwilling to let it go to waste.

I watched them eat, watched them start to relax, and prepared for that moment when comfort led to relaxation…

Led to tears.

It started with Anne, a slight catch to an exhaled breath, and then a hiccup in the following inhale. Her eyes widened, and then teared up. Kelley got hit with the maelstrom of emotion next, mouth stuck open in an attempt to take in the air her panic was denying her.

"Hey. It's ok." I was up and moving and pulling my chair over between them. "It's ok. I've got you." And I did. I lightly wrapped an arm around each girl, letting them feel it there but not restraining, not constricting. I let them make the next move, allowing them to decide what comfort they wanted or needed. Kelley leaned into me, a sob shuddering its way free of her thin frame. Anne stared at me, eyes wide, tears and snot starting to run as her breathing grew erratic and stressed. "I've got you. Honest."

They were too young for this. They were thin, they were exhausted, and they were stressed and terrified to this choking, sobbing point where a kind stranger was the straw that broke their tough facade. Fuck this miserable shitty world and the people who broke it and broke each other.

I wanted a drink, and I didn't even drink.

We sat there until exhaustion overwhelmed whatever horror they were processing. Until breathing and heart rates relaxed and both girls were leaning into me. I curled my arms around them.

"I've got you."

* * *

I HAD NEVER WANTED KIDS, but it was nice to have Kelley and Anne around. They were siblings, maybe. Possibly close relatives. They were obviously familiar with working together, being together. There is a sort of unconscious communication that develops between people used to moving through the same space.

That collaborative awareness moved them through breakfast and out into the garden. They needed direction in a garden they were not familiar with, but they seemed to know plants well enough to not weed the scraggly tomato plants out of their raised bed. That was good enough for me. I dug at the pea bed, wondering just how all of this dock and evening primrose had managed to get established without my noticing. I kept an eye on the sun. If it got much higher the temperature would become a bit unbearable and the sun a bit too much to handle. Best get what we could finished up soon.

"Thank you." Anne's voice was quiet, tentative, as it broke the easy silence of our gardening.

I didn't look up, just sort of waved a dirty hand in their direction. The relief and gratitude in her voice made me uncomfortable. "I should be thanking you. It's been a while since I had a hand on the farm."

"Really, thank you." It was Kelley's turn to make me uncomfortable. "We...things were bad. Thank you."

"Things are better now, I hope." I wiped at my face with the cleanest part of my forearm, trying to get at an itch.

"Unless you are going to try and sell us, yes. Much better."

I didn't really need, or want, to know I had been right. Fuck people. Selling, kidnapping. The world went to shit and everyone just decided to fuck each other over. I was never the neighborhood Welcome Wagon sort of person, but I liked that vague sort of sense of community that came from casual nods and shared bitching about the weather. Drought, hose bans, usage caps, and then once there were so many rules trying to manage so little resource everything just sort of toppled over. No more causal nods. No more letting your kids out to play in the dust.

Don't go outside, the Stoats will get you.

Don't be too loud, the Stoats will find you.

Hush now.

"Family?" I asked casually, finally looking up, looking at the girls.

"Uncle and Aunt. We didn't see them very much and were excited they were visiting." Kelley trailed off.

"'Visiting' really is a different sort of word now, isn't it?" I spoke more to try to tamp down my temper than to start an actual linguistic discussion. No one just visited anymore. There was always a reason, hidden or otherwise. Learned that one the hard way myself...and I was not going to chase that train of thought any further.

"So. I am not at all interested in selling you on. You don't have to worry about that. Far as I am concerned you are part of the farm here. It's work, but I could use the help in exchange for the water usage, safe space to sleep, and food to eat. If that sounds good to you, come on in for a drink out of the sun. We have shit inside to do while the sun is out here cooking everything." I paused. "I swear. A lot. The chickens don't seem to mind, and it has become a habit. That's just a thing you get to deal with." I didn't wait for a response before letting myself in through the utility room door. They would follow me in, or they would scarper. Either way I was thirsty. I put out two extra glasses just in case.

* * *

ANOTHER STORM ROLLED through that afternoon as the girls were working on organizing a truly desolate corner of the house for me— the Hoard of Mason Jars. Thunder rumbled through with its promise of rain, and the hair on my arms stood on end. I hoped the storm would not miss us. Water use for three (and some chickens) was more than water use for one. I needed to work out rations and plans and really pay attention to water collection. The well was deep and reliable, so far, but the rain was not. I stared out the window at the darkening sky.

Boot, one of the remaining roosters, sounded an alarm from the front of the house. Could be a hawk, another damn dog, a falling leaf. Roosters were both really good and absolutely terrible at what they do. Boot called again, the sound getting cut off at the end before the hens started shouting. Hens screaming and roosters choking on their own shouts was normal background music for the farm.

I took care of my tools, even the ones I used rarely. I picked up an old and beloved tool as I opened the front door and stepped outside. The sound of a flock of birds overreacting was normal, but today I trusted their judgement, and raised the old rifle with practiced ease as I left the house. I was nicely prepared to greet the man standing over the body of my second-to-last rooster, bloodied knife in hand. His arms were scratched.

Good boy, Boot.

"Afternoon. Kindly get the fuck off my farm." I smiled in a way that made sure to show my teeth. It tasted more like a snarl than a smile, but I was trying to be polite. "You owe me for the roo."

"I think you have something of mine, so I consider us even." His smile was just as unfriendly as my own, and then crueler. It twisted through the muscles and form of his face, but it failed to make its way to his eyes. Those mud brown eyes seemed bored. Bland.

"Nothing of yours here."

Don't go outside, the Stoats will get you.

Don't be too loud, the Stoats will find you.

Hush now.

Hush.

The old rhyme was always running in the back of my head. I had whispered it to Angie over and over so she would memorize it, so it would become the rhythm that guided her through surviving each day. Hush. Hush. Be quiet and small. Don't let them find you.

Fuck lot of good that had done.

"I know they are here, the Sheldon girls. I followed them." The Stoat tried another smile on. It fit just as poorly as the previous. "Their da sent me."

"Oh, like hell he did." I could see a bit of the girls in the shape of his eyes and the sharp cheekbones. This must be the uncle.

There used to be rules about things. No cutting in line. Tip your barista. Don't steal. And definitely don't kill. There had been delicate threads strong as spider silk holding the entire shit show together. Sure, those threads, that web, got strained every now and then, and sometimes a big gross bug struggled free and made a mess of things until we rebuilt. But that careful web spun from a need for cooperation, empathy, and acceptance rested at the core of society. All society. Dig down deep enough through culture and religion and you can find those common threads, those familiar rules.

Desperation was a terrible thing. We had all been so desperate for water that we had torn right through that careful web and discarded it. I could see desperation in the eyes of Uncle Sheldon. It haunted the faces of Anne and Kelley. It kept me steady as I raised my rifle and shot once. It allowed me to ignore the surprise in Uncle Sheldon's face as he fell.

I was a good shot. I had to be.

Hush now.

Hush

"See, Angie? I'm a much better shot now."

The girls must have heard the shot and would hopefully have

gone to ground. They didn't need to see this. My girls. "I've got you," I whispered.

I couldn't rebuild what had been broken. There were no rules of conduct, no web of community anymore. Everyone looked after themselves. I had enough water. I had a bit of land. I was willing to kill to keep it. I had my own little web I worked with, I had a little family again to look after. My hand didn't shake as I cleared the chamber and set my rifle aside.

Zombies would have been easier. We could have worked together against that threat. Could have arisen from the bloodied ashes and rebuilt. A desperation for water and resources would be the death of us all. It had taken my sisters from me. My Angie. It had killed the man on the ground in front of me.

Like hell I would let it take the girls.

ACKNOWLEDGMENTS

I tell my students that nothing exists in a vaccum. That there is always a step back you can take and more context to take in. There is a crowd of context that exists here, cozy and close to this book.

From the folks that have taken a chance on me and published my work, like Blaze Ward and Leah Cutter, to the folks who are willing to look over rough and rushed drafts and help me coax them into something beautiful like Sarah Eaton.

Then to the person who keeps reminding me the Good Work is always worth doing, Laura Anne Gilman. I am pretty sure I would have thrown my hands up in defeat, in many arenas, without her encouragement and equally necessary snark.

I will always hold deep love and gratitude towards Snow Leopard Clan and the deep work we all did atop our mountain, each supporting the other. I needed that.

And of course the person who listens and reassures and comforts and challenges me and urges me always to be better, at my craft and as a person, Ben.

The cats obviously run this show, and deserve a place in the acknowledgements. But they are more interested in what is in the treat cupboard and I am sure won't bother to take a look here.

I haven't mentioned so many of you. I don't have the space, not in a library of books, to express my gratitude and love and laughter. So, simply, thank you. You. Yep, I mean you. You know what I am talking about.

ABOUT THE AUTHOR

April Steenburgh is the pen name of Burdock Broughton. They live on a homestead near the shore of Lake Ontario with a cunning little cat they found in a swamp. That cat might be a witch. They share their homestead with four other foundling felines, a small herd of alpaca, some chatty goats, a roving horde of chickens, one very friendly turkey, and a very understanding husband.

April has published multiple short stories and does not intend on stopping any time soon. When not writing, April can be found working as an eSports coach and English professor. They also make soaps and salves as Twigloo Farms.

April manages Faery Cat Press with fellow author Laura Anne Gilman.